A Snowfall Valley Novel

K.E. Monteith

Also by K.E. Monteith

<u>Standalones</u>
All Grown Up
Third Time's The Charm
One Dropped Key
Quitting My Boss
Gym Daddy

<u>Snowfall Valley Series</u>
Back When We Faked It
Strike to Burn
A Much Kneaded Union
Crushes & Christmas
Snapshot Problems
Dirty Charisma Check
Give Me a Redo

ASIN: B0CNZFXNCP

Amazon ISBN: 9798872258384

Ingram ISBN: 9798869025289

Cover design by: Acacia at Ever After Cover Design

Town map by: Book and Mood

For my boy, who let's my crazy shine

Contents

AUTHOR'S NOTE

Please note that this book contains sexually explicit scenes, heavy mentions of a cheating ex, moderate depiction of loss of a parent, and a minor scene with an officer/sheriff that does not end in conflict

Snowfall Valley

NORTH CAROLINA

THE
PLAYLIST

- Should've Said No - Taylor Swift
- Life Is A Highway - Rascal Flatts
- Whose Bed Have Your Boots Been Under? - Shania Twain
- Picture To Burn - Taylor Swift
- I Want Crazy - Hunter Hayes
- Take A Bow - Rihanna
- Miss You Being Gone - The Band Perry
- Stars - Grace Potter & The Nocturnals
- Best Thing I Never Had - Beyoncé
- Not Ready to Make Nice - The Chicks
- Watch - Billie Eilish
- Bless The Broken Rode - Rascal Flatts
- I Like to Be With Me When I'm With You - Drew Holcomb & The Neighbors
- Now The We Don't Talk - Taylor Swift
- Don't Start Now - Ingrid Andress
- Doomsday - Lizzy McAlpine
- Lady Like - Ingrid Andress
- Heartbroken - Diplo
- Hey Stephen - Taylor Swift
- Feel Like This - Ingrid Andress
- Forever And For Always - Shania Twain

ICYMI

The Snowfall Valley Series is a set of interconnected standalones. You don't have to read them in order if you don't want to. Here's all you need to know for Zoey & Stephen's story

- Zoey has been with her high school sweetheart, Johnny, for over 10 years
- Lately, Johnny hasn't been around at events he normally attended with Zoey
- Zoey has been spending more time in her auto shop, frequently coming to hangouts covered in grease and grime and a bad attitude
- After a spat with her best friend, Olivia, Zoey admitted she thinks Johnny is cheating

1

BLOWJOBS AND VINTAGE CARS

ZOEY

I couldn't stop my knee from bouncing and it was pissing me off. This bastard didn't deserve my concern. He deserved to be pushed into a pile of shit. He deserved salt in his wounds, washed out with salt water, and coated in more salt. That fucker deserved to burn.

And despite all that, my gut was twisted into so many damn knots that I couldn't breathe. Because even though I shouldn't, even though I hated that I did, I still cared about Johnny. I cared about him so damn fucking much. And that made everything burn twice as badly.

"Zo!"

My head shot up to see Roxie damn near sprinting across the hospital waiting room in death heels. I jumped out of my seat to meet her halfway because it was the least I could do for ruining her New Year's Eve plans, whatever they may have been. And definitely not because I needed the hug that she offered.

"What's wrong? Where's everybody else? Are you okay?" Rox squeezed me tightly before pulling away and looking me up and down.

"I didn't text the others," I mumbled, trying to turn away. But Rox didn't let go of my shoulders. She squeezed tighter, raising a perfectly shaped eyebrow.

This was another reason Johnny deserved to be shoved into shit. I now had to tell everyone what he did. *Me*, not him, *me*. And with every single person I told, I'd have to face the pity. Again and again, until everyone in town knew.

Suddenly I regretted convincing Olivia, my best friend, to stop working at the Paper and pursue a career that actually made her happy. At least then she'd be able to save me from one form of small town gossip. I wonder what McKree will have to say about this. Would he focus on the no-good bastard or me? Will the patriarchy win or his common decency?

"Why didn't you tell anybody else?" Roxie asked, voice hushed.

I bit my tongue. I wasn't ready to say it out loud yet. It hadn't *technically* been confirmed. All the person who'd called me said was that Johnny was in the car in a 'compromising' position with another woman when he crashed. Compromising could mean anything.

I didn't believe it meant anything but the obvious, but if it let me hold off saying the exact words. I'd hold on to that as tight as fucking possible.

"I need to get tested. And you're the one who knows about that shit. So, you know …" I really wish she wasn't still holding on to me. That way I wouldn't have to watch her face as she processed what I said. The widening of her eyes stung.

But they didn't soften into pity like I feared. Instead, her grip tightened, nose flaring. "Where is he?"

"Getting stitches and a caste." I shrugged out of her hold and went back to my chair to grab my bag. When I turned back, Rox was looking at me with wonder. It only took a second for me to realize what she thought had happened. "I didn't do it. I haven't spoken to him yet."

I honestly had no idea what I would say when I saw Johnny. There was no excusing his way out of this one. He'd have to admit it. And I'd have to … do something.

"All right. So ... do you know how long until you can see him?" Roxie asked, refocusing me.

"I dunno." I looked over to the doors where a nurse or surgeon or whatever had gone after telling me the basics of Johnny's procedures. Beyond the fact that he wasn't in serious medical trouble, I didn't absorb much. "Maybe an hour or so."

"Right," Roxie said definitively, looping an arm around mine and pulling me to the front desk. "Evening ..." Rox glanced at the woman's name tag before continuing, "Lacey. My friend and I need some general STD tests, please."

"You're getting one too?" I asked at the same time Lacey asked, "Names?"

"Roxanne Davis and Zoey Riggs," Roxie answered. Then she turned to me and squeezed my arm. "And of course. I won't let you do it alone."

Fuck I loved my friends.

"Any changes to insurance or addresses for either of you?"

"No," we answered. Then Roxie added, "And if Johnathon Clark can take visitors while we're testing, can you have someone let us know?"

Lacey clicked through a few things on her computer before asking, "Relation to the patient?"

"I'm his ... emergency contact," I answered, that shaky feeling coming back. It was rage and anxiety and the feeling of everything in my life breaking down. I fucking hated it. What did I do to deserve this?

"Oh," was all that came out of Lacey. Roxie's hand found my arm again, giving me a comforting squeeze.

I was desperate to ask the nurse what that 'oh' meant. I wanted to know everything and nothing and crawl into a hole and never come out.

But there was one thing I could ask that wouldn't send me into a spiral.

"Do you know how the car is? The '66 Chevy Corvette?" There was probably a good bit of damage considering the dumbass broke his arm.

But I could fix damn near anything. And if I couldn't, I knew somebody who could. And that kind of project was exactly what I needed right now. Something I could focus on, something that I didn't need to talk to anybody to do.

"Oh," Lacey repeated. And my gut sank for a second time that night.

"**Y**ou wrecked my '66 for a fucking blowjob?"

Johnny didn't have the sense to look ashamed when I stepped into his room. He didn't shy away from the accusation or fiddle nervously with his hospital bed sheets. He didn't turn red or scratch the back of his neck, which were his usual tells.

Instead, Johnny sat there, staring at me with a furrowed brow, which must've stung given the line of stitches across his forehead.

"What're you more mad about? Me cheating or wrecking the car?"

There it was. Confirmation of what I'd suspected for the last few months. Stated so simply too.

It took two or three steps to get from the door to Johnny's bed. And it took one deep breath to smack his smug, beautiful, hateful face.

The sting in my palm lasted one single heartbeat.

One heartbeat. Everything was done in one single fucking heartbeat.

It took a bit longer for them to escort me out of the hospital.

2

DESPERATE EVASION OF ENDANGERED
RASCALS

STEPHEN

"I told you to take a vacation, Stephen. Not take the street view car out to gather more data," Darren grumbled over the car speakers. I should have known better than to answer his call. But I'd been on the road for almost a week now and I was starting to miss my best friend.

"Your workaholic ways are a pain in my ass. This little field trip isn't in the budget, you know."

I missed him even if he was a bit of a prick sometimes.

"Good to hear from you too," I mumbled under my breath. I glanced up to my rearview mirror to see a car quickly approaching. I hit my blinker, moved into the right lane, and let him pass. There was barely anybody on the roads, so I stayed in place, letting cruise control take over. I'd never done such a long road trip before, but I was coming to find I liked it. The quiet, the endless road. It was peaceful.

"I'm just saying, do you even know the meaning of taking a break?" Darren asked and I couldn't help but chuckle. It'd been like this since college. I'd be doing work and Darren would arbitrarily decide I needed a mental health break and drag me away. And even though we were business partners and full-grown adults now, not much had changed.

"I'm testing the scenic route option. You know, the thing we made specifically for vacations." I didn't mention that I was driving through areas we had limited data on. He probably already assumed that's what I was doing anyway.

"Dude. I need you well rested. For the company and your general well-being. What happens if you overwork yourself and crash? Or you get stuck in the middle of nowhere and start having a panic attack because you can't work?"

"I have my laptop with me. Obviously."

"Not the point, Stephen. I'm worried about you. Where even are you right now?"

I glanced over to the monitor to my right to confirm I was nowhere near a big, recognizable city. "Somewhere in North Carolina. Along the mountains."

"North Carolina? You drove all the way across the fucking country?"

"I've been gone for a week."

"You've been gone for five days. Have you been making stops?"

"Of course, I have."

"For more than just sleep?"

I bit my tongue, knowing he wouldn't like the answer. I really shouldn't have answered his call. It was getting late, the roads were dark, and I needed to find food and a place to stay soon.

"Christ. Well, seeing as you're *literally* across the country, can you at least promise me one thing?"

Since Darren wasn't one to settle so quickly, I jumped on the compromise. Even though I should have known better.

"Sure. What?"

"Stay some place for more than one night. See some sights. Be an obnoxious tourist. Do something that isn't even tangentially related to work. You can do that, right?"

I was about to tell him he was being dramatic. That I'd done plenty on my cross-country trip that didn't involve work.

But then something skittered into the road, demanding all my attention.

My first thought was *there's no way that's a real deer, it's* fucking *huge.*

My second thought was, *fuck, I'm gonna kill it, I don't wanna kill it.*

The deer in question remained frozen in the middle of the road, my headlights reflecting bright panic in his eyes. Panic I shared. Panic that told me the best course of action would be to jerk to the right and slam on the breaks.

Panic that sent me straight into a tree.

The impact felt like somebody sat on the remote, turning the TV to a channel of static. Everything was fuzzy and all I heard was buzzing.

And then the airbag erupted and everything went white. And musty.

I didn't do anything at first. I sat there with smelly fabric pushed against my face, the sound of breaking glass ringing in my ears. I sat there and internally screamed until my mental voice was hoarse.

And when I'd collected myself, I smacked my way through the airbag to grab my phone and get out of the car.

As soon as my door opened, the deer's head turned to me. He was still in the middle of the road, head cocked like he was curious about what I was doing. As if I hadn't just wrecked my car and endangered myself for him.

"You could say thank you, you know?" I told him. To which he shook his whole body before sprinting back into the woods he came from. It was impressive speed given that he hadn't moved an inch to avoid an oncoming vehicle.

"STEPHEN OSCAR GILL, ANSWER THE FUCKING PHONE!"

Oh right, Darren.

"Sorry, there was this deer," I explained once I put the phone to my ear.

"Jesus fucking Christ, man. Are you all right?"

I took a second to look down at my body, brushing away a few shards of glass, but not finding any injuries other than the bruise on my knee from when I ran into a table at an antique shop the other day. The store had this odd sign about stocking the most tables in America and I'd gotten curious. It wasn't as impressive as I thought it'd be.

"I'm fine."

"Are you sure you're fine? Because I just heard the crash and had a fucking heart attack." Darren was a good friend, overbearingness and all.

"Yeah. It really wasn't that bad. I just swerved to not hit this deer. He was huge. I mean, *huge*. Do you think they keep deer as pets in the South? That's the only explanation for why that deer was so big."

"Are you sure you didn't hit your head man?"

"No, really, you need to see this deer. We probably got him on camera." I leaned back into the car and tapped at the monitor. It was, of course, dead. As was the dashboard and the radio and the inside lights. "Fuck."

"What? What happened?"

Ignoring Darren, I walked around to the front of the car to take in the damage. The front was completely crumbled, nearly wrapped around a tree. And the camera on top of the car was literally hanging on by a chord.

"No, no, no," I shouted, dropping my phone to fumble up the remainder of the hood and grab the camera. Darren continued to screech from my phone, but I was focused on making sure the camera and its various lenses didn't take any more damage. The car might not be an easy or cheap fix, but the camera would be ten times worse. Which was something our startup couldn't afford.

Once the camera was detached from all its chords and safe in the back seat, I went back to grab my phone.

"I think I saved the camera. We'll probably need new chords though, most of them snapped. And the front of the car is completely wrecked." I took a hesitant step toward the engine to get a better look at the damage.

I didn't know much about cars, but I knew enough to know smoke was a bad sign. Didn't smell like pancakes though. "It's if the smoke smells like pancakes that it's gonna explode, right?"

"Stephen, get the fuck away from that car," Darren shouted instead of answering my question.

"It's not that much smoke. And it doesn't smell like pancakes."

"Please, for the love of god, don't base your safety on something you read on the internet once. Get away from the car."

"I will. Just let me get my insurance card. And wallet. And bag."

"Jesus fucking Christ. I'm gonna have to figure out how to get your body shipped back to Washington, aren't I?"

"That sounds like a waste of money," I told him, reaching into the car to grab my things on the passenger seat. There was an odd clinking sound coming from somewhere in the car, A metal tap, tap, tapping. I grabbed the rest of my things in a hurry.

"Darren, I'm hanging up now to call for a tow. I'll confirm I didn't die later."

"Oh, thanks. Sorry if it's such a hardship for you to —" My thumb swiped to end the call before he could give me any more attitude.

With Darren out of the way, I took a deep breath and really looked around the area. It looked identical to every other section of road I'd driven on today. Two lanes, minimal streetlights, and lots and lots of trees.

But there was one distinguishing thing. A blue sign listing a mechanic at the next exit. Bright neon letters in the middle of a gear spelled out 'Zoey's Shop'. Well, at least that's one thing solved.

After a thirty-minute wait on the phone and another ten-minute wait on the side of the road, I was picked up by a quiet man who brought me and my car to an auto shop in a little shopping center. There was, possibly, a restaurant named Cal's, a craft store, a nail salon, and a large grocery store with one letter of the store sign out.

"Oh shit, is that a street view car?" a woman's voice exclaimed once I'd stepped out of the car. The driver, who'd also gotten out and rounded the vehicles to start undoing the clasps, grunted an affirmative.

"That's so cool. Can I check out the cameras?" the woman asked, taking long steps from the open garage door to my car. Her face was smeared with different shades of grease or grime or something. Her hands were covered in the same way. But she was ... bright. Or maybe that was just the way the neon shop sign reflected off her blonde hair.

"Where is it?"

"What?" She was right in front of me, bright and shiny and distracting.

"The camera. Can I see it? Or did it get lost in the crash?"

"Oh, no. It's in the back. Most of the chords snapped when I hit the tree. From a branch or something. But I was able to disconnect it before the camera fell." The woman, whose name tag said Zoey, stepped passed me and opened the back door.

She was awfully cute. And apparently the shop owner. And maybe a mechanic herself. It was unclear.

"This is so cool," she murmured from the inside of the car. Then she pulled out and rested her arm over the car roof. "So what happened?"

God, how did I forget that deer already?

"There was the huge —"

"Deer," we all said at once, even the man who'd driven me here, and he'd barely even taken my name when he picked me up.

"That's Clive," Zoey explained, "He's sorta a local .... rascal. He's got a habit of hopping out into the road and endangering himself and others." She laughed like something about this deer causing trouble was funny.

"Shouldn't animal control put him down or something if he causes that much trouble." This had the woman turning to me with the most 'what the fuck' look I've ever seen. I immediately backtracked. "Sorry. I didn't mean —"

"Nah, it's all right," Zoey said, shaking her head and moving away from the car. "He's sorta like a town mascot, so we've got a soft spot for him even if he causes trouble. We'll do a once-over of your car here and get you an estimate in an hour or so. If ya haven't eaten yet, I recommend Cal's. Thursdays are margarita nights."

With nothing else to do, I grabbed my bag and headed to Cal's.

3

DEPRESSION MEETS A DRUNKARD

ZOEY

"It's time to make the call," Dan grumbled. He was crouched to my left, tilting his head to see what I'd been doing under the car. A whole lot of nothing is what.

I don't know why I thought a street view car would be different under the hood than anything else, but it wasn't. It was an ordinary car with a camera glued on top, nothing exciting or distracting about it. And it was fucking wrecked. We'd need to replace the frame and damn near everything under the hood. Clive really did a number on this guy. I should really start sending him a commission for all the work he got me. Maybe carrots or whatever the fuck deer eat.

"Fine," I grumbled, sliding out from under the car. "How many of the parts do we have on hand?"

Dan looked away.

"Fine. How long will it take to get all the parts in?"

Dan, still looking away, mumbled something under his breath. I stuck my foot out to hit his shin.

"A week if he's willing to pay expedited shipping."

"Christ, all right." I sat up and rested my arms on my knees. "Well, he's gotta work for Google or some shit, so at least his boss'll have to pay for it. I'll go let him know."

"Go?" Dan repeated while I stood and wiped grease off my hands and onto my knees.

"He headed to Cal's, right? I'll go break the bad news to him and you can call Tracy to see if there are any rooms available." I left Dan grumbling at the front desk and crossed the parking lot to my favorite restaurant in Snowfall.

My favorite because you can never undervalue reliable queso within walking distance. And because I always got a laugh at tourists' whiplash when they discovered the restaurant they assumed to be generic American food was actually Mexican.

I walked around a family in the front whisper arguing over whether they actually wanted Mexican or not and walked up to the hostess stand.

"Hey Carla, I'm looking for a client of mine that came in here around an hour ago. White dude, kinda looks like a scrawny version of that guy from Smallville. You seen him?" I asked, leaning on the counter as I spoke.

"Oh, yeah, that guy," Carla said, stretching out the words in a way that made me immediately suspicious.

"God, what'd he do?"

"Oh, he didn't really *do* anything. He just — well, he's at the bar. Go see for yourself." Clara pointed over her shoulder at the center bar and then turned back to the arguing family who was ready to be seated.

Not sure what to expect, I headed to the bar. And as soon as I saw him, I understood what Carla meant.

Stephen was slumped over the counter, surrounded by an open laptop and five empty margarita glasses. With his head on the counter, he typed into his computer, mumbling something I couldn't make out. Next to him was Louis, an older man who started coming to Cal's to watch games when

Mason turned the Pub into a cafe. Louis patted Stephen on the shoulder before moving to close the man's laptop. Stephen shot up, shouting.

"No, no, no. I gotta try to recover the picture. I have to show Darren the deer. He didn't believe me."

"Son, I've got plenty of pictures of Clive I can give you. Now put the laptop away and enjoy the game." With glazed eyes, Stephen looked from his screen to the small TV over the bar. Small being the operative word.

"What game is that?" he asked, squinting his eyes and leaning over the counter. He pushed up, standing on the footrest of his stool, and I decided that was my time to interrupt.

I stepped on the footrest on the other side of the stool so he didn't fall forward. The stool thunked back to the ground and Stephen fell into my arms. Literally. He stared up at me, hazel eyes wide and very clearly wasted.

"Hey, Stephen," I said, doing my best to make my smile friendly and not like I was about to deliver bad news.

"Zoey?" Stephen said my name like he didn't believe it. He must've been way past wasted.

"I've got some bad news for ya, bud," I said, helping him get righted on the seat. "We don't have all the parts in stock to fix your car. It'll take a week to get 'em. And that's *if* you're willing to pay for expedited shipping."

Instead of the rage or general frustration I expected at the news, I got a blank stare. Stephen was so quiet, I looked to Louis to confirm I'd actually spoken words out loud. The older man just shrugged and turned his focus back to the TV.

"Hey, Stephen?" I prompted, resting a hand on his upper arm. His eyes met mine for the briefest of seconds before he threw his head back and groaned.

"Darren's gonna kill me. All because I didn't want to hit a deer. If I hadn't stopped to look at antiques yesterday, this never would have happened. I wanted to be in New York by tomorrow."

"Dude, you would've had to drive for ... I dunno, definitely over ten hours to get to New York from here." Probably not the most important thing in that little rant of his, but a good note nonetheless.

"Okay, then ... Pennsylvania. I could be in Pennsylvania tomorrow if I hadn't gone to the antique shop. Maybe Maryland. I want to test the scenic routes more. There're a lot of blank spots in Virginia around the mountains."

"Okay, Stephen, you're a bit too drunk to be planning routes. Let's get you back to the shop and find somewhere for you to stay tonight." I started packing up his laptop and waved for the bartender.

"No, no, no. Darren said something about ... hmm, maybe having fun? Drinking is fun, right?" The words were slow and slurred and I considered giving the bartender shit for letting this dude drink so much.

"I mean, have you been having fun?" I asked, sliding his computer into his bag. From the register, Tim held up a card I took to be Stephen's. Well, at least the dude had the sense to open a tab. Not sure if he'd eaten though.

"Not really. Darren kicked me out of the office, so I thought I could fill in the gaps in our GPS. But I've fucked that up." The guy slumped over, face flat on the sticky surface of the bar, lip pouted. "I bet I made him worry even more now."

I didn't realize men could be so cute.

"Sounds like a good friend. Why don't you call him and let him know you're all right."

"I did," Stephen puffed out. "He yelled at me."

"Ha! Sounds like a really good friend," I laughed, just as Tim came around with Stephen's card and receipt. While Stephen signed, I threw his bag over my shoulder and turned to the bartender, "Tim, why'd you let him drink so much, man?"

"He knew all the trivia questions," Tim said with a shrug before taking Stephen's signed copy back to the register.

"You knew all the trivia questions?" I asked. Tim had a book under the bar and would pull from the harder sections the more drinks you had. And they got tough. I'd gotten through three drinks once and my trivia was to name the first 20 digits of pie.

"They were pretty basic questions," Stephen mumbled, clicking and unclicking the pen. I took it and set it down out of arms reach.

"All right, time to go. Think you can walk across the lot, bud?"

"Hmm," Stephen grumbled. He pushed back against the counter and stood. There was … an amount of wobbling. "My legs feel like jello."

"Not a great sign," I murmured, taking one of his arms and draping it around my neck. I waved goodbye to Louis, then slowly guided Stephen out of the restaurant and back to my shop.

Dan was waiting outside for us, his usual frown deeper than normal.

"Oh shit, what is it?" I moved Stephen's arm off me and set him on the curb. He sat, then immediately curled up into a ball mumbling something too quiet and slurred for me to understand.

"Taylor weddings got Tracy's all booked," Dan answered, arms crossed, eyes narrowed at Stephen. For his part, Stephen moved to slide his bag off my shoulder and used it as a pillow to lie down with.

"Shit." I looked down at Stephen, then back to Dan. Well, it wasn't my idea of a good time but having someone to take care of would be a helluva lot better than what I'd been doing lately. Which was mostly staring at Johnny's leftover shit and alternating between crying and screaming. "I'll take him home then."

"What?" Dan asked, straightening.

"Well, what else are we gonna do with him? I've got a spare room, so it's not a problem."

"Yeah, but …" Dan trailed off, looking around before saying, "You're living alone now."

It stung every damn time I remembered Johnny. It stung even worse when somebody else reminded me of him.

"You really think *that*," I pointed to Stephen half asleep on the ground, "is gonna hurt me?"

"Well, you never know," Dan huffed and I rolled my eyes.

"Come on, Stephen, we're having a sleepover." From the ground, Stephen shot up, looking around in a daze.

"Just ... make sure you lock your bedroom door, all right?" Dan said, taking my arm before I passed him to get back into the shop. I knew he was saying that because he cared about me, but it felt like he didn't think I could care for myself. Which was fucking ridiculous. Even when Johnny wasn't a bitch, I made more money, I owned the house, the cars.

But, I knew what Dan meant. So I swallowed down the never ending anger and agreed.

4

Happy and Ecstatic to Reluctant and Scared

Stephen

I kept my eyes closed for as long as possible for several reasons.

One, I had no clue where I was. For all I knew I could be in a booth at Cal's. And while I was certain Darren would get a kick out of this predicament, I knew this wasn't what he meant by 'act like a tourist'.

Two, my head was spinning. A solid argument for staying in place.

Three, the one thing I could remember was wrecking my car. There was no way that cute mechanic could fix it overnight. Unless she was magic, which when I remembered her eyes, seemed possible. Either way, it was just another problem I didn't want to face while hungover.

All of those problems could be dealt with after a few more hours of sleep.

Except I really had to pee.

Fuck.

Fine, I'll find a bathroom, piss, then go right back to sleep.

Surely wherever I was had a bathroom.

I cracked my eyes open just enough to confirm I was in a bedroom. A homey bedroom. Maybe a B&B. But any desire to examine my surroundings was quickly smothered by the way my bladder shifted as I sat up.

Shit, when was the last time I pissed? Had I gone since the rest stop a few hours before the crash?

With squinted eyes, I rushed out of the bedroom and tried the first door I saw. Linens. Next door. Toilet.

Thank fucking god.

I rushed to throw the lid open and pee. Relief rushed through my body and I suddenly realized a few key details about my surroundings.

The shower next to the toilet, where I was standing with my dick in my hand, was running. The shower was running and somebody on the other side of the shower curtain, probably naked, was stifling a laugh. And they were failing miserably.

"You all right there, dude?" a woman asked from behind the curtain. Still laugh when she added, "You just kinda stopped mid-stream there."

To my mortification, it was then that my body decided to finish peeing. Or maybe it was a panic response and this sort of embarrassment would have made me pee my pants had I been wearing them.

"I am *so* sorry." I stumbled over the words, rushing to put myself away and give the presumably naked woman her space back.

"No worries. After all those drinks, it's no wonder you woke up needing to piss."

"Zoey?" I asked, frozen in place, pants up, hand on the lever to flush. Memories came in flashes. The cute mechanic coming into the restaurant. Her wrapping my arm around her neck and carrying me away.

And apparently, bringing me into her home.

"Glad you're not so hungover that you can't remember that," she laughed. "And don't flush. Old house, shitty pipes, you know? Also means if you want a shower, you're gonna have to wait a bit for the water to heat back up. Also-also, I was thinking pancakes for breakfast. How's that sound?"

I set down the toilet lid, questioning reality. Was everything really spinning or was that the hangover? Was the adorable girl I met yesterday really showering and talking to me like it was a completely normal thing or was I dreaming?

I needed to sit down.

"Hey, Stephen? You still there, bud?"

"Yes." I sat on the toilet, cradling my head in my hands. "Pancakes sound nice."

"Cool. I'm not sure what I have in terms of toppings, but feel free to look around the kitchen."

"Okay." This was so confusing and weird and my head hurt.

The shower curtain crinkled and my eyes shot up to see Zoey's head. Just her head. Not that I wanted to see the rest of her.

No, I did, just not right now or not like this. Or maybe not at all. I wasn't sure.

Her hair was soaked, darker and wavier than it was yesterday. She squinted at me, blue eyes so fucking bright as she looked me over. I think my heart was in my throat. She really was so cute and pretty.

"Why'd you sit down, weirdo?" she teased, a smile pulling up her lips. I was struck with the thought that she was also a really nice person too.

And I was staring at her in the shower.

"Shit, sorry." I shot up, turning away and rushing out of the bathroom. Zoey's laughs echoed behind me as I shut the door.

I stood there for a minute, trying to wrap my head around the interaction. But after a few minutes of thinking, I decided there was no understanding it. Certainly not in my current state.

So I retreated back to the bedroom. Looking around the room now, I found my phone, plugged in, on the bedside table and my bags stacked neatly on the dresser. My clothes and shoes from yesterday were in a clump at the edge of the bed. The realization that she'd just seen me in my underwear and I'd likely stripped in front of her last night, sent a new wave of embarrassment through me. Fucking hell, she should have just let me sleep in my car for all the trouble I must've caused.

Reaching for my phone, I immediately called Darren, because that's what I did when I had trouble understanding people.

"Dear fucking lord, Stephen. Do you know what time it is?" was Darren's immediate answer.

"No. But I've got a problem."

"If it's the fact that you wrecked the car or that you're immensely hungover, I'm aware of both issues. A mechanic's looking at the car and you can sleep the hangover off."

"I'm at the mechanic's house." I've known Darren long enough to tell his silences apart. This was a 'you're not making any sense, did you accidentally take drugs?' silence. "I remember she came to the restaurant and I guess she brought me to her place."

"Her?" he exclaimed.

"Examine your biases."

"Yeah, sure. I'll examine my biases after you tell me if you slept with the mechanic or not."

"No, I woke up in the guest room. I think." I went over to the dresser to find every drawer empty. "Definitely the guest room. Can I talk about my thing now?"

"Christ, you do know I'm three hours behind you, right?"

"That's not an answer." Darren let out a heavy sigh that I took to mean I could go on. "So I woke up not really knowing where I was."

"Great start," Darren murmured. I ignored him.

"I tried to go back to sleep to avoid my problems. But I had to piss. So I got up to go to the bathroom."

"Naturally." I continued to ignore Darren.

"And as I was peeing, I realized the shower was running."

"Oh shit."

"And Zoey, that's the mechanic's name, she just ... talked to me. Like it was normal. She asked if I was okay with pancakes for breakfast. All while she was *showering* and I had my dick in my hand. That's not normal, right?"

Darren's reply was laughter, which was entirely unhelpful.

"Darren," I hissed. "What do I do?"

"I dunno, man. Apologize and eat some pancakes, I guess. Maybe brace yourself to get slapped. What'd she say?"

"Nothing, really. I got dizzy and confused, so I sat down and she called me a weirdo. But she ... she was teasing me. I think."

"Interesting."

"What do you mean interesting?" I pressed. I should be getting dressed, not holding my breath for his answer. But the whole situation was ... I don't know, it knocked me off my feet. Not that I was on solid footing with most people, but this felt different. Probably because no one had ever taken me home like a stray puppy before.

"Tell me more about this Zoey."

Maybe talking to Darren was a waste of time. I refocused my energy on fishing out clean clothes from my bag, only half paying attention to my answer. "She's a mechanic. Cute. A little shorter than me. Maybe your height. Blonde hair, blue eyes. The soap she was using was citrusy. I think she might be the owner of the shop. She had a lot of grease on her face the other day, so she definitely works on the cars herself."

"*Interesting,*" Darren repeated.

"What?" I asked, a tad sharper than necessary. But I hated when he said cryptic shit like this. And he knew that.

"I think you're attracted to her."

"Well ... yeah, she's cute. Anyone would be attracted to her. But what does that have to do with her talking to me so casually while she's showering?"

"Oh. Sorry, dude. Probably means she's not interested."

I halted my process of getting dressed, pants around my calves.

"That's ... irrelevant."

"Uh-huh. If it was irrelevant, then you wouldn't be feeling awkward. You might be the smartest person I know, but you're a dumbass when it comes to social interactions. If you weren't attracted to her, you probably wouldn't have even noticed the shower situation was weird."

"That's not true," I argued and continued getting dressed. Darren didn't know what he was talking about. I was plenty socially aware. Or at least aware enough to know that talking to someone while their naked was odd.

"Yeah, sure. And you just happen to care enough about this to call me at this ungodly early hour because ..."

"I walked in on a woman showering," I shouted. "That's a big deal!"

"I mean ... she didn't seem to think it was a big deal, right?"

Before I had the chance to argue with Darren any further, there was a knock at my door. I hung up on Darren without another word and opened the door.

"Oh, hey. Wasn't sure you'd answer," Zoey said taking a few steps back in surprise when I threw the door open.

"You knocked, why wouldn't I answer?" I tried to will my brain to not focus on Zoey the way Darren claimed I was. It didn't listen. Instead, I was unable to tear my eyes away from the nape of her neck, where small drops of water trailed and pooled around her collarbone. She hadn't dried her hair, but put it up in a clip, loose waves falling over the plastic like a waterfall.

"Well, given your state of confusion a bit ago, I figured you might need some more sleep."

"No." Many people took issue with direct answers, especially short *and* direct answers. There was no reason to believe Zoey was any different. But as I was summoning up the words to explain myself further, she shrugged.

"Yeah, sure, all right. You can help me with the pancakes then." And with that, she turned and walked down the hallway. I followed.

The kitchen reminded me of a cottage. The whole house had a cottage aesthetic really, but the kitchen made me think it was intentional. Dandelion yellow cabinets and wooden countertops made the room feel warm and cozy. Several porcelain containers were already lined up on the counters, chalk labels on each. Zoey grabbed a towel that matched her eyes and threw it over her shoulder before turning to me.

"So, plain or chocolate chips?" she asked, tilting her head to a bag of chips on the counter.

"Plain."

Zoey's lips twitched up like maybe she expected my answer. "Thoughts on small talk?"

"I'd rather not."

Again, she smiled like she knew what I was going to say.

Smitten. I was smitten. Crushing on this strange woman and her bright smile and her lack of small talk.

Zoey pulled out her phone from her back pocket and the country twang of Rascal Flatts filled the air. The one from *Cars*. She sang along, hums and words blurring together as she swayed around and turned back to the counter. As she began measuring ingredients and pouring them into a mixing bowl, my eyes began to drift. They drifted along the slope of her back, the cropped shirt she wore exposing delicate skin. And ...

Fuck. Darren put the idea in my head and it made everything worse.

I pushed the useless thoughts away and looked around for something to do.

Dishes. I could clean dishes.

"Oh, thanks," Zoey said as I stepped up to the sink and began cleaning the few plates and utensils there. Unfortunately, while doing the dishes made me feel useful and kept my hands busy, it also put me right next to

Zoey. And there was something very ... mouth-watering about her orange and honey scent.

"No, I should be thanking you for taking me in. You could have easily left me at that restaurant."

"Sure, but then I would've felt bad if I went back to the shop and found you sleeping in your car." She bopped her hip into me, a small knock of our bodies that made my nervous system scream.

"Um, yeah. Thank you." I focused on scraping at a bit of food on a plate and once it came off, my nerves had calmed a little. "About the car ..."

"Oh shit, you don't remember, do you?" Zoey's hands paused stirring the batter before she broke the bad news. "I don't have all the parts needed to fix ... everything under the hood really. And even if we expedite shipping, it'll take a week to get here. So ... not exactly cheap. But at least your boss'll cover it, right?"

I let the news sink in, let the dread settle in my bones. Then I stared at the ceiling and sighed.

How had one deer caused so much trouble?

"I'm the boss. Well, me and my friend. We're a startup. Sort of. And ... how long would it take for standard shipping?" I turned to look at Zoey, who was grimacing down at the batter.

"Two to ... six weeks. That's what you get for having a foreign car," she murmured, returning to mixing. "We could also find you something used and fix it up with the camera and shit. It'd probably cost more, but it'd save you time. Dan's running the shop solo today, so I'll have him run a price check for all ya."

"Whatever's the cheapest. I've got my work laptop, so at least I won't fall behind on our deadlines. After breakfast ... and maybe a shower, I'll check in to the nearest hotel." Hopefully, the hotel stay wouldn't cost more than the expedited shipping. This place seemed like a small enough town to not be a tourist hot spot. Maybe I could spring for a B&B. Though a chain hotel might have a more reliable internet connection.

"Another bit of bad news on that front," Zoey said, cradling the mixing bowl in her left arm and moving over to the stove. "There's a wedding in town this week for the Taylor's oldest grandkid. Ms. Taylor is like … the unofficial community leader here. And her family is Irish Catholic, so the motel is all booked for the next couple of days. You're welcome to stay here or I could drive you out to the next closest hotel. I think it's —"

A knock at the door made Zoey pause and her whole body went rigid. The response seemed odd, but given that I'd only spoken to her for an hour at most, I brushed the thought away. Until a harsher knock came and the tension left her shoulders. Not that she relaxed, but more like she gave up.

"One second," she murmured, abandoning the mixing bowl precariously on the counter. It teetered and I threw my arms out to catch it just in time for it to spill over. Thick batter covered my sleeve and the floor as I struggled to right the bowl, every edge of it too slippery to grab.

And dear lord, how many pancakes did she think the two of us would need? A good cup or two or maybe even five had fallen onto the floor and the bowl was still nearly full. And so much of it was on my clothes, seeping through the fabric and making my skin crawl.

They had to go.

If anyone was around, they might've questioned if my clothes were on fire given how fast I threw them off. But I just couldn't *do* mushy items. They made me gag. I'd rather face my high school nightmares of taking a test in my underwear than let the batter touch me anymore.

Plus Zoey had already proven she was unbothered by seeing me in my boxers, so what did it matter?

Clothes now balled in my hands, I looked around for signs of a washer. Seeing none, I folded my clothes so the batter was on the inside of the pile, and set them on the counter before heading out of the kitchen to find Zoey.

It wasn't a hard search. As soon as I turned out of the kitchen, I heard angry whispers at the front door. There, Zoey stood in front of a man, tall, blonde, swooped-back hair. His arms were crossed, rolling his eyes at whatever it was Zoey had said. Zoey's hands clinched by her side.

I got the distinct impression she wanted to punch him.

"Everything all right?" I asked, stepping up behind Zoey. She shifted to the side, just enough to look at me, rolling her eyes.

"It's fine, he's just being an asshole," she mumbled, all her brightness and sharpness dulled.

"And who are you?" the man asked, eyes narrowed as he looked me up and down.

There was something about this guy, the way he was regarding Zoey, the way Zoey seemed like a diluted version of the woman in the kitchen just minutes ago, that made me instantly dislike him. And since Zoey seemed to want to get rid of him, I did the first thing that came to mind. Pretend he was interrupting something intimate.

Stepping closer to Zoey, I wrapped an arm around her waist and pulled her against me. Then I answered the asshole's question.

"Hers."

The man's face twisted, his eyes darting to Zoey. I couldn't see her face, but whatever she did must have been convincing. The man's face reddened, eyes snapping to me, full of anger.

"Is that so? Didn't think you'd bring someone home so quickly, Zo."

In my hold, Zoey tensed. I pulled her even closer, my thumb stroking the soft skin of her exposed stomach.

"I think you should go," I told the man, forcing his attention back to me. But he only spared a moment to glare at me before returning to Zoey.

"I need my things, Zo."

"Well, I gave you an hour to collect your shit from my house. So I don't see why it's my problem."

"It's my *birth certificate*. I need it for my new job," the man argued. Zoey shrugged in my arms and said nothing.

"How about you go and we'll look for it?" I suggested, my fingers sliding under Zoey's waistband to have something to hold onto. The man looked angry enough to throw a punch and that made me nervous. Would I be able to move quickly enough so that Zoey didn't get hurt?

"There's no need to look for it. She knows exactly where it is." The man's eyes zeroed in on my hand, nostrils flaring.

"Is that true, Zoey?" I asked, pulling her flush against me so I could meet her eyes when she tilted her head back. Those blue eyes were wide in the poorest attempt at innocence I've ever seen.

It was kind of endearing.

"If it wasn't with all the other official documents, then I don't know where it is."

"But you wouldn't tell me *where* you put all that shit," the man growled. And while sure, Zoey was being a tad difficult, it was hard to believe a grown man wouldn't know where something like his birth certificate was.

"Well ... like I said, we'll look for it. *After* you leave." Again, the man glared at me before finally huffing and stepping back.

"Bring it to the Pub tonight. Your little boyfriend too. I'm sure everyone'll wanna meet him. Hope he's good at trivia," the man spat. I wrapped my free arm across Zoey's stomach, keeping her close as she jerked towards him, a fist raised. But the man didn't look back, not to glare at me or catch a glimpse of Zoey.

"God, he's such a fucking asshole," Zoey murmured once the man had gotten into his car and driven away, her body relaxing into me.

"An ex?" I guessed. My thumb on her stomach subconsciously rubbed small circles against her skin, the touch soothing. She didn't push me away, so I kept the movement up, matching her breaths.

"Yeah. Twelve fucking years and he cheated on me. *And* wrecked one of the cars I rebuilt with my dad before he passed." There was so much vitriol in her voice that you'd think it was the reason for every bone in my body freezing up.

But it wasn't.

I froze because it made no logical sense for that man to have cheated on the woman in my arms. And the only thought that came to mind, which I found myself voicing, was, "Why?"

Zoey tilted her head back again to look at me, a bitter smile making her eyes glisten. "Why'd he cheat? Or why'd he wreck the car? Because the answer to both is, apparently, a good blow job."

"Do you not do them?" I asked, regretting the words immediately. But instead of cringing or yelling at me, Zoey threw her head back, thunking into me, and laughed. It was a crackly kind of laugh, her eyes squinted, sharp smile lines forming. It was very cute.

"I guess not good enough," Zoey said through a laugh before stepping out of my hold. My hands fell to my side, empty. She turned to face me, an eyebrow raised. "So ... what happened to your clothes?"

"Oh, right." I looked down at my boxers and then around Zoey's neighborhood. Some folks across the street were on their porch, clearly watching the show. "The pancake mix fell and I don't do well with that sort of texture. I was coming over here to ask where the washer was."

Zoey placed a hand on my shoulder, guiding me back inside. Once the door was closed, she stepped away from me and towards the kitchen.

I found I preferred it when she was touching me.

"Got any more clothes that need washing?" Zoey asked as she walked out of the kitchen, my clothes in hand.

"Oh, yes." I followed her down the hallway, ducking into my room to grab my bag, then continued following her to the washer. As I dumped my clothes in, she measured out detergent. Laundry in, Zoey leaned over me to turn the dial and press a button. And then we stood there, silent.

"So ..." Zoey said after a few seconds of picking lint off her shirt. "Think you could pretend to like me for a night?"

"I do like you."

Zoey jerked, knocking into the washer as she turned to asses me. The words had just tumbled out, but I hadn't thought them to be ... worth a reaction. Zoey was nice, cute. She quite literally took me in when I had nowhere to go. There were only reasons to like her.

"Oh," Zoey said, clearing her throat. "Well, then I guess that'll make pretending to be my boyfriend tonight easier."

I nodded, because yeah. I couldn't imagine pretending I liked her on a romantic level would be all that hard. And I wasn't doing anything else anyway.

"Great." Zoey hopped in place a little, straightening her back. "Then you go get dressed and I'll finish making the pancakes."

5

FRIENDS WILL WORRY NO MATTER WHAT YOU DO

ZOEY

Me: I did something mildly questionable

Me: No follow up questions

Olivia: Zoey you can't just text shit like that and not send the thing you're gonna say immediately after!

Rosie: It is quite worrying, sweetie

Shea: I love unhinged Zoey

Me: So Clive fucked up this dude's car and he got drunk at Cal's while waiting for the assessment, so I let him crash at my place

Olivia: ZOEY!

Rosie: Shea, you live closest can you check on her?

Shea: Yeah, this is a level of unhinged I can't support

Me: I told you no follow up questions

Me: Let me finish

Olivia: You can't text in bits like that and expect us not to react

Me: ANYWAYS, Johnny came over to get some shit and this guy helped me out and is gonna pretend to be my boyfriend at trivia, so you know, I need you all there pretending you know and like him

Shea: Huh, wonder where you got * that * idea * big eyes *

Olivia: oh my god, it was one time!

Shea: It was twice!!!

Olivia: … fine.

Olivia: But it was only one guy

Shea: Twice

Rosie: Can you tell us a little bit about this man?

Rosie: Shea, maybe you should pop in. Just to make sure

Me: Oh my god, he's fine. Had he wanted to try anything, he would've done it when he walked in on me in the shower

Rosie: He did what?!?!

Shea: I'll be over in a bit, I'm at Wheelz

Shea: Olivia, Denny says to eat lunch

Olivia: Oh fuck off

Rosie: What happened in the shower?!?!

Me: Nothing! He was just hungover and half asleep and had to piss. He did the whole deer in the headlights thing when he realized I was there and left like a good boy

Roxie: I do love a good boy

Shea: Dead

Ashley: When you say you need everyone at trivia, you don't mean me, right?

Me: Everyone means everyone

Shea: Consider it espionage

Ashley: ugh fine. But you owe me

Me: Yeah, yeah, your next oil change is free or whatever

Rosie: Sweetie, name, please

Olivia: Yeah, give us a name so we can stalk the shit out of him

Me: Stephen …

Olivia: Oh my god, you let this man stay at your house without knowing his last name

Me: The motel was full from the Taylor wedding

Ashley: That wedding is the bane of my existence. Chelsea has changed the cake flavor five times

Me: It's Gill

Me: He says he doesn't really do social media

Olivia: Did you tell him we wanted to stalk him?

Me: No, I just asked what his username was, figured that'd save you some trouble

Roxie: I found his LinkedIn, he's got some sort of tech company

Roxie: Nerdy-cute, I like that. The nerdy ones tend to be pleasers

Me: Him and his friend are making some sort of advanced GPS thing. The car he wrecked had a street view camera

Me: It wasn't as cool as I thought it'd be

Me: But Stephen's a nice guy, a little awkward, but I like him

Roxie: RE

Roxie: BOUND

Roxie: SEX

Roxie: !!!

Olivia: I dunno, Rox

Rosie: It might be a good idea

Roxie: THAT'S MY BESTIE

Ashley: Never thought I'd hear that from you, Rosie

Shea: Rosie's a secret hoe, that's why her and Roxie are so close

Rosie: oh hush, you two. I just think that there's no harm in a nice, consensual night to relieve stress

Roxie: I'll bring condoms to the Pub

Roxie: Does he have BDE?

Shea: So do I need to go over and check on Zo or what?

Me: No

Rosie: Yes

Me: NO. I'll see y'all at the Pub

Me: And don't embarrass me, this dude is gonna be in town for a few weeks waiting for a part

6

TWO FAKE DATERS ENTER A NOT PUB, THEY MIGHT KISS (THEY WILL)

ZOEY

"**A**ll right, repeat that back to me."

"I'd really rather not," Stephen said, a look of horror twisting his lips as we walked towards the Pub.

He had kinda full lips for a dude.

Which *didn't* matter.

Roxie's demand for rebound sex was just getting to me. That and Rosie's support of said rebound sex. I must've looked pretty damn pathetic if she was trying to push me into bed with a stranger. Though I guess that was better than her insisting this was some meant to be meet cute. For once, Rosie wasn't romanticizing something.

"Just the names then."

"Olivia, your best friend, and her partner, Dennis. Rosie owns a diner, Shea is the funny-blunt one, Roxie is … I'm uncomfortable repeating what you said."

"I didn't say anything bad," I said, nudging into him. "She's just comfortable expressing her sexuality."

"Sure, but you get how that would sound bad coming from me, right?" Stephen paused for a second, looking around at the downtown strip we'd entered. As I kept walking, he crossed behind me to stand on the other side of me, closer to the road. Weirdo.

"Fine, Roxie is … the first person I called after shit went down."

Stephen narrowed his eyes at me, but he didn't comment or ask any follow-up questions.

"So Roxie is reliable. And Ashley is a baker and hates the owner of this pub we're going to, so I should keep an eye on her. Am I missing anyone?"

"Technically, Bailey. But she lives in Charlotte now and has been kinda MIA in the group chat."

"You miss her?" Stephen asked, slipping his arm through mine and pulling me out of the way of a passerby. When they'd passed, Stephen kept his arm in place and tucked his hand into his coat pocket.

His question was innocent. The kind of follow-up question anyone would ask. But Johnny never asked those questions. He didn't do follow-ups or ask about my feelings or friends. He could barely ever remember Ashley's name.

But this stranger did.

And it pissed me the fuck off.

How could Johnny do that? Live with somebody for over five years and not ask about them and their friends? Claim you love them and not ask the most basic questions?

And how did I let him get away with it?

I don't know who I was more disappointed with, Johnny or myself.

"Sorry. Was that too personal?" Stephen asked. He began to pull away, but I pinned his arm to my body. We were close enough to the Pub now that we needed to keep up appearances. And it was cold as fuck for February. Those were the only reasons I needed him close. Not because the way my orange soap mixed with his natural musk made me want to snuggle into his neck.

Fuck, is this what being touch-starved does to you?

"No, I just got stuck thinking about stupid shit. I do miss her. Thanks for asking."

"Yeah. Um ..." Stephen leaned in closer, his breath ticking my ear, and asked, "Are we on now?"

"What a weird way to say that," I snorted.

"You call me that a lot," he noted, squinting at me like he was trying to figure something out.

"Well, you are kinda weird, aren'tcha?" I nudged him a little but he only shrugged, so I added, "I like weird though. So you're in good company."

At that, Stephen smiled. A warm, kinda boyish smile. Then he opened his mouth to say something and was immediately cut off.

"Hey, Stephen! Zo's told us so much about you!" Roxie shouted, flinging her arms around me and Stephen in a tight hug. Beside me, Stephen stiffened. His free hand went to Roxie's shoulder and he gently pushed her away.

"Sorry, I'm not big on touching," he murmured with his arm still tightly wrapped around mine.

"Oh my goodness, sorry. I should've asked. Roxie, by the way. Nice to formally meet you," she said, waving. I watched Stephen to see if he did what every guy did around Roxie. For his eyes to fall down her body, for the nervous ticks, all the other weird shit guys did to impress a girl.

"Nice to meet you too. Are the others in the pub already?" he asked, polite, cordial even. He didn't gawk or stammer. He didn't look at her with any sort of desire. And he looked back at me, held me even closer, almost as if he could see the insecurity running around in my head and took its hand so it'd stop doing laps.

It was weird. Unsettling. Comforting.

"Yeah, we've got a table in the back-ish. Ashley is making spitballs and aiming them at hard-to-clean places. Shea is helping," Roxie said as she led us into the Pub.

"That tracks," I said while Stephen, in horror, murmured, "Spitballs?"

"She's using water ... I think."

Stephen shivered.

We meandered our way through the crowded cafe and I kept my eyes focused on my friends in the back the whole way. I could hear the shift in conversation, feel folks' eyes on me. I'd avoided going out to town events for well over a month now because of this. The nauseating pity. The whispered assumptions. The quick look to where Johnny and I normally sat when he deigned to come to trivia.

It made me want to throw shit.

"You all right?" Stephen asked, leaning closer to whisper in my ear.

Ahead of us, Roxie paused, an eyebrow raised. I hadn't mentioned this was my first time out in the group chat. I didn't have to, the girls knew. I was a hundred percent certain they discussed this tactic of getting me through the crowd with as little ruckus as possible. And it was all wasted because even the looks were getting to me.

Fuck it. Fine. I'll give them something else to stare and gossip about.

I turned, grabbed Stephen by the collar, and pulled him into a kiss.

To some extent, I was aware of the crowd around us. The way whispers shifted. The way Roxie clapped and Shea hooted.

But mostly I was aware that this was the second man I'd ever kissed and I was comparing everything to Johnny. Stephen's lips were softer, like maybe he actually used ChapStick in the winter instead of just licking his lips over and over and making the problem worse. Stephen didn't smell like cars, which was something I'd always associated with comfort and home. But it was nice not being overwhelmed by that smell. Like a breath of fresh air.

And most strikingly, even though his tongue passed over mine, his kiss wasn't hungry. It was tender. It was a soft touch, a moment of connection. Something I hadn't felt in so damn long.

It burned.

Stephen pulled away, his hand sliding down my arm to intertwine our fingers. He gave me a funny sort of look, squinted eyes and tilted head. He leaned forward and pressed a soft kiss to my forehead. The action ... comforted the anger, tucked the emotion into bed so it could rest, even if just for a minute.

I stared at Stephen like he had grown an extra head. He might as well have for being able to quiet my emotions like that. For his part, Stephen didn't respond to my wild eyes and crooked look. He just took me to my friends and we were quickly engulfed and those feelings were pushed to the side.

"Hey, Stephen!" everyone cheered once we reached the table. Folks shuffled out of their seats, taking turns to give me a hug and Stephen a wave or handshake. Each time I let go of a friend, my hand found Stephen's again, giving it a quick squeeze before hugging the next friend. It wasn't something I really thought about until I saw Olivia clock it as she stepped back from our hug and Dennis took his turn.

"You all right, Zoey?" he asked, hands on my shoulders as he looked me up and down. I rolled my eyes and pushed his hands away.

"I'm fine. It's not like I'm the first in the group to fake kiss somebody," I grumbled, taking my seat at the high-top table, Stephen sitting to my left and Olivia on my right.

"Shush," she hissed, nudging me in the stomach. "That was different. At least I knew Dennis beforehand. He wasn't some stranger off the street. No offense, Stephen."

"What's happening?" Stephen asked, once again leaning over to whisper in my ear.

"They fake-dated in high school and then again a couple of months ago," I said, pointing to Olivia and Dennis.

"And ... is that a normal thing for this town?" Stephen asked, eyeing everyone at the table as if he was looking for someone to confirm two fake dating couples at one table was an insane coincidence.

"No," Olivia and I answered. While on the other side of the table, Roxie and Shea said, "Yeah."

The two idiots with one brain cell high-fived.

"It's not," I assured.

"Are you sure? Because this town has a deer mascot."

"Clive isn't our mascot. Zoey's just obsessed with him because he makes her money," Olivia scoffed.

"Okay, but Clive did hook you two up," Shea pointed out.

"Wait, what?" I asked, turning to my best friend who was so red in the face, she nearly matched her hair.

"Shea forced me to go get some things from the shed on Thanksgiving and ... Clive locked us in. Neither of us had our phones so ..." Olivia trailed off and Roxie threw her head back laughing, the others quickly following suit.

"Why didn't you tell me?" I whispered, pulling Olivia close. On my other side, Stephen held onto my arm, keeping me balanced on the seat as I leaned into my friend.

"I don't know, you were ..." Olivia trailed off, then shrugged. I knew why she hadn't said anything. I'd been in a pissed-off, shut-down mood the whole time she'd been going through her crisis and indecision with Dennis. I'd been a shit friend. And the consequence of that was missing out on pivotal best-friend talks. Like being locked in a shed because of a deer. My favorite deer.

"There are a lot of coffee options for a pub," Stephen murmured and Ashley jolted upright.

"You thought it was a pub too! See!" she shouted.

"No one said you were crazy for thinking the Pub was a pub," Shea said, putting a hand on her shoulder.

"It's a perfect reasonable mix-up," Rosie added.

"Wait, is it not a pub?" Stephen asked, turning to me for an explanation.

"Not anymore. When Mason took it over from his grandfather, he changed it to a coffee shop/cafe type thing."

"Without changing the name!" Ashley chimed in.

"Wait, so this place is called the Pub? You weren't just saying the pub in town?"

"All the older stores in town are named literally. There's the Paper, the Market," Dennis answered with a sigh.

"So this is a hallmark movie town?" Stephen asked and I knocked into him with my shoulder, trying to glare at him while resisting a grin.

"Shut up," I grumbled, nudging him again.

"There was actually a rumor they were gonna film a hallmark movie here. But the lead pulled out before they got anywhere," Rosie said.

"Was it anyone cool?" Roxie asked.

"Hmm, the name sounded familiar, but I can't remember who it was."

"Y'all wanna order anything? Triva'll start in 20," Travis said, tapping his notebook on our table as he stepped up between Stephen and me. While the rest ordered, Stephen reached past Travis to grab my hand. It seemed like overkill for the fake dating game, but surprisingly I didn't mind it. It was cute how hard he was working to play the part.

"Where is he?" Ashley said when Travis got to her order. The man tilted his head back and sighed. And then he saw the spitballs on the ceiling and sighed again.

"Ashley, I'm begging you not to start any trouble tonight. You're worse than my five-year-old."

"I don't *start* anything. He does. *He* filled my dumpster with his stupid ass coffee boxes yesterday."

"Well, he's not here tonight. So behave," Travis said, giving her a pointed look. And as much as I wanted to give him credit as a single dad, the look was far too weak to discourage anyone. Let alone his son, Jayson, who had a bit of a wild streak.

"Where'd he go? Pretty irresponsible to not be present for his business's event."

"I dunno. Went off with some girl. Now do you want to order anything or not?"

There was a brief moment where Ashley froze, her face paling a fraction before she pulled herself together. Olivia nudged my side and we exchanged a look. In theory, Ashley should be nothing but relieved to hear Mason wasn't around.

But not a single one of us in the friend group bought that theory.

Especially not when Ashley shot out of her seat and sped off somewhere.

We looked around the table, each concerned but a little scared to check on her. Ashley had a tendency of getting *real* defensive if we so much as implied she had any feelings other than hatred towards Mason. And if we questioned her retaliations against him? Forget it. We'd be without leftover baked goods for a week. And none of us wanted to lose that privilege.

Though honestly, it might feel good to take a page out of her book. Get a little revenge for all the crap Johnny'd done.

"I'll check on her," Rosie said, pushing away from the table and following off after Ashley.

I turned to watch Rosie go just as the front door opened and Johnny walked in.

Trivia was a monthly thing at the Pub, a tradition carried over from its pub days because the older folks demanded it. Johnny and I'd started coming with my dad once I'd moved out. It was our bonding night. And after Dad passed, it was our date night.

Now Johnny came in surrounded by his boys.

And I hated the part of me that was grateful there wasn't a woman on his arm.

Except then the door opened again and there she was. The woman who gave a blowjob so good the bastard crashed one of my most prized possessions.

A squeeze on my hand brought me back to earth.

"What's our trivia team name?" Stephen asked, pulling me so I had to turn away from Johnny and his mistress.

"Oh, Shea's normally the one who comes up with the names," I said, pointing over to my friend, who was preoccupied with Denny. In fact, everybody was occupied. Nobody had noticed Johnny stepping in and sending me into a quiet, murderous rage. Nobody but Stephen.

"I don't like the way you looked at him," Stephen murmured, tapping the pencil Travis dropped off with the trivia card and our drinks.

"How was that?"

"Something between murderous and depressed." Stephen's eyes drifted to Johnny, who was grabbing at the woman's ass as they made their way across the restaurant to *our* usual table. Stephen's hold on my hand tightened. "Let's do something about it."

7

Trivia Revolves Around Malevolent Prattle

Stephen

It was hard to explain why seeing Zoey look at Johnny with so many warring emotions unsettled me so much. But I guess it could boil down to the fact that I like Zoey. She was kind and brusque and didn't deserve that pain.

And maybe that kiss did some rewiring of my brain.

It was hard to tell surrounded by this hallmark-esque small town with all its drama and quirks.

"Do something, huh? Like what?" Zoey fully turned towards me, knees against my thigh, head tilted.

"Well first, let's not give him a reason to talk to you. Give me his birth certificate and I'll give it to him." I held out my hand to Zoey before realizing she hadn't been carrying anything when we left her house. She rolled her eyes and tilted to the side to pull a folded sheet of paper out of her overalls.

"Zoey, did you seriously fold up his birth certificate?" I asked, causing her friends to whip around with wide eyes.

"Zoey!" Olivia shouted, snatching the paper from Zoey and trying to straighten out the folds with the table. Beside her, her partner laughed and rubbed her back. It was the sort of soft intimacy that supposedly felt natural for everyone else, but I'd never experienced it. Even when I'd been with someone I'd wanted that connection with, I could never get to that point where casual touches were comfortable. The only person I'd ever been that way around outside my family was Darren, and he wasn't my type.

"Ashley, what the fuck were you doing up there?" Travis yelled from the not-bar as Ashley and Rosie reappeared from a hallway on the opposite side of the restaurant.

"Nothing that'll cause you any trouble," Ashley grumbled as she was pushed back towards our table by Rosie. When she passed Johnny, the man narrowed his eyes at Zoey's friends before looking over at me and Zoey.

Nasty was the only way to describe the look that Johnny was giving us.

I slid my hand through the side of Zoey's overalls and under her sweater. Her head swiveled to me, blonde waves bouncing across my chest. Ignoring her look of confusion, I rested my forehead on hers and pressed her as close as I could without pulling her off her stool.

"Remember, you have to pretend you like me," I whispered. Our faces were so close that when she giggled in response, our lips brushed.

"I do like you, weirdo." She pushed me playfully before turning back towards the table. But she didn't move my hand from under her shirt. "Of all the folks Clive has crashed, you're my favorite."

"So what'd you do, Ashley?" Shea asked when the other woman returned to her seat.

"Just get the whiskey out, Shea," Rosie murmured, nearly collapsing onto her stool.

"God, you're acting like I murdered someone."

"You broke into his apartment!"

"She what?" the table shouted, even me. We all leaned into the table, wide eyes pointed at Ashley.

"How'd you get in?" Zoey asked.

"There was a key under his mat. Figured the man was dumb enough to do that sort of thing."

"So you just went in and …" Olivia said, arms crossed on the table, nearly folded over it as she leaned closer.

"I turned off all his alarm clocks."

"By?" Rosie prompted, arms crossed and giving Ashley the most mom look I'd ever seen.

"By cutting the chords."

"And?"

"And," the others repeated.

"And I might have dumped most everything in his kitchen into the sink." Ashley shrugged, crossing her arms and leaning back against the wall.

"You could be arrested for breaking and entering," Rosie screeched.

"Kinda sounds like a waste of food," Shea noted, pulling out a bottle of … whiskey from somewhere below the table. She poured some into her coffee, then held out the bottle for the others.

"What could he have possibly done to deserve that?" Olivia asked while Dennis poured some whiskey into his and Olivia's glasses.

"I should take a page out of your book," Zoey said, pouring a shit ton of whiskey into her glass, taking a big gulp, then pouring some more.

"Is this allowed?" I asked when Zoey, after taking another swig, handed me the bottle. She nodded, so I poured a bit and passed it along.

"What do you mean?" Ashley asked.

"I mean I should do the shit you do to Mason to Johnny. He sure as hell deserves that much."

Beside me, Roxie passed the drink to Rosie without taking any, and Rosie poured herself a small dash before the bottle disappeared under the table.

"I don't know, Zo," Roxie started but Zoey shook her head.

"No. That fucker deserves it. What else have you done to Mason?" Zoey snatched the trivia card and pencil from me, flipping the card over and writing 'revenge' in all caps at the top.

"Um ... a couple of weeks ago, I told one of the delivery guys he was out of town and he didn't have to-go cups for a week."

"You should just key his car," Shea said and Zoey jerked, a look of disgust wrinkling her face.

"I would never. I love that car."

"Guess putting glitter in the air vents is out of the question too, huh?" Ashley said.

"Did you do that?" Roxie asked.

"What about magnets?" I asked, all eyes turning to me with a suddenness that suggested the girls might have forgotten I was there.

"Whadaya mean?" Zoey asked, blue eyes wide and ... a little hopeful.

"Well, you don't want to damage the car, so you could make a car magnet instead. Hell, if you don't care about the money, you could get enough to cover the whole car."

"Could you design that for me?" Zoey asked Olivia. The other woman's mouth twisted and she leaned back into her partner.

"I don't think that's —"

"He deserves it after everything he did to me!" Zoey shouted and the whole cafe quieted.

From across the room, I could see Johnny sneer and roll his eyes.

Hands on Zoey's shoulders, I turned her to face me, taking her face in my hands.

"You're right. He does." Tears formed at the edge of her eyes. "I'll do whatever you come up with while I'm here. He'll get what he deserves. Promise."

"Really?" she asked, a little breathy, like maybe that big gulp of whiskey was already going to her head.

"Of course." I could feel her friends eye me, sizing me up, assessing my motives. But there really *wasn't* any motive. It was just the right answer.

"Even if I wanna spread a rumor that he's gay and has several STDs and a micro penis?"

"Well ..." I started, but fortunately Zoey's friends stepped in for that.

"Zo, let's examine that gay line," Shea said, standing on the footrest of her stool to lean over and bop Zoey on the head.

"And the STD thing," Roxie added, leaning over me to nudge Zoey too.

"Fine. What about the micro penis thing?" she asked and all eyes went to Dennis and me.

"I don't think you should," I said, my words hesitant.

"Yeah, feels wrong," Dennis added. The women looked at each other, then shrugged in unison.

"You should focus your insults on skill-based things," Ashley said.

"Yeah, like when was the last time he made you come?" Roxie asked and all the girls leaned in to hear the answer. Zoey leaned forward, elbows on the table, and sipped her alcohol-laden coffee as she thought. And thought. And thought. And thought.

And as she thought, the cup emptied and she leaned against me, tilting until she was almost in my lap. I wrapped my arms around her, keeping her steady on the stool. Her eyes were so bright, but distant as she looked up at me.

"I dunno. Sex just sorta ... stopped being fun years ago. Most of the time I'd rather be in the garage working."

"Do you think that's because you weren't connecting with Johnny or because you just don't want sex that much?" Roxie asked, leaning closer to me to look at Zoey. But Zoey's eyes didn't leave mine.

"No, I definitely want sex. I just don't wanna feel ..." Zoey's hand reached up, cupping my face. I wanted to look away, to look at her friends and confirm I wasn't encouraging this or doing anything even a bit close to scummy. But I couldn't tear my eyes away from Zoey and the storm brewing inside her. "I don't wanna feel like I'm pretending anymore. Like it's always work."

I covered her hand with mine and said, "You don't have to pretend here. You're with friends. ... and me."

Zoey snorted, a bright smile lighting up her face.

It was relieving to see.

And just as I was about to tell her that or that her smile was nice or something of the like, the sound system blared.

Shania Twain filled the room with a loud twang, asking her lover who else he'd been sleeping with and all eyes turned to Johnny. The man paled for a moment before red engulfed his face. The woman he was with scooted her stool further away, eyes on the table. Meanwhile, his friends whistled and hollered, patting him on the back for being a 'mangy dog'.

"The simplest revenge is never letting him forget what he did," Ashley said, holding up her phone as it played the song connected to the Pub's speakers.

"Oh man, if Bailey were here, she'd have us line dancing," Shea said, wistfulness softening her voice.

"Line dancing?" Ashley repeated, face scrunched. Zoey jerked up and hopped off her stool, a hand stretched out to her friend. Ashley hesitated for a second before sighing and taking Zoey's hand. They took off to the back side of the bar, Olivia and Shea following close behind them, where they pushed back a few armchairs and the coffee table to make a pseudo dance floor. While Zoey walked Ashley through a simple routine, the other two danced around in a complicated series of circles and hops and claps. The women were all smiles and giggles and mocking each other's poor coordination. But even in that moment of happiness, I saw Zoey's eyes flick to Johnny and watched her brightness dim.

"So," Roxie said, stretching out the word as she scooted closer to me. "What are your intentions with our dear Zoey?"

"What?" I stammered.

"Rox, go easy on the poor boy. He's gotten dragged into a real mess," Rosie said, pulling at Roxie's arm to give me more space.

"I'm just curious. I mean, you saw the look she gave him."

"The look?" I asked, hopeful that they could explain it because I was desperate to know what it meant.

"Oh, you know the look. So what're you gonna do about it?"

"Sweetie, I think she's just a little tipsy. You know Zoey's a lightweight."

Sure, but like, that wouldn't make her give a look like that if she didn't already feel some type away."

"Well, sure, but he didn't give *her* a look. You can't force this just to move her grieving along faster."

"No, he did though. He doesn't like touching."

"Yes, you told us."

"But he was holding her hand on the way here. And you saw how he slid his hand under her shirt."

"Johnny was looking over here."

I turned to Dennis, hoping he'd provide some break to this mild argument. But his eyes were glued to his girl. So I followed his example and watched Zoey. Her movements were loose and silly. Enchanting.

A few other folks had joined the girls. An older couple swung together and another friend group screamed in a corner. And Johnny still glared at them.

I should be dancing with her.

The music died and all eyes went to the bar. There, Travis tapped on a microphone, eyes narrowed at Ashley. "If you're done causing trouble. It's time to start trivia."

The crowd grumbled but returned to their seats. The girls walked back slowest, Ashley giving Travis a dirty look as she passed. If that was how she treated an employee at her rival's store, I'd hate to see how she acted around this Mason guy.

"All right, now everyone's got that out of their systems, who's playing?" Travis asked and several hands shot up, including some at Johnny's table. Not his though, he seemed to be too busy getting handsy with the woman he came in with.

"Team name?" Travis asked our table, speaking into the microphone.

"Pumpkin Eaters!" Shea shouted.

"Pumpkin eaters?" the rest of the table repeated.

"Yeah, like that phrase cheater, cheater, pumpkin eater."

"But wouldn't that make us the cheaters?" Olivia asked.

"... saying the phrase out loud, I realize I've misunderstood something."

"Wait, what were you thinking?" Ashley asked.

"That pumpkin eaters eat cheaters."

"We're team Pumpkin Eaters Eat Cheaters, Travis!" Roxie yelled.

"I'm not saying all that. I'll call you all pumpkins," Travis said before turning to the next group. Shea, Roxie, and Zoey booed but quickly quieted down when Shea brought the whiskey back out.

Trivia went by in a blur of shouts and giggles and drink after drink. Our trivia answers were spelled progressively worse and between Ashley and Zoey, the back of our trivia card and three napkins were filled with different revenge plans, each one more ridiculous than the last. Some of which were certainly illegal, but Ashley promised she could get Zoey out of any legal problems.

Despite the ridiculousness of the whole situation, the unfamiliar atmosphere, the strangers, I found myself having fun. And when our team was handed a plastic trophy and Travis was given Roxie's phone for a picture, my smile was genuine.

Though, if pressed, I'd have to admit my happiness was directly tied to Zoey. The way she smiled around her friends, the way she laughed without holding back, the way she said the most unhinged shit without a hint of remorse. And the way she touched me. She'd squeeze my arm when we got an answer right. She'd laugh into my shoulder when somebody made a particularly bad joke. She'd slide her hand under my shirt and gently rub circles into the sensitive skin of my waist and press kisses into my arms. And sometimes those kisses crept up to my neck while her hand fell to my thigh.

All those little touches left me hungry. *Starving* for more, more of her smiles, more of those giggles, more of those moments of light banishing the cloud over her head.

Plus there was that look. The look where she couldn't remember when she last came. The look where she said she wanted sex while staring right at me. Those looks strengthened the hunger.

But so did the drinks.

We need to sober up before going back to her place.

"Are you done with these games now, Zo?" Johnny asked, walking towards our table, his friends at his back. The other woman was noticeably absent.

"You mean are we done beating your ass? We got the trophy, so I guess so," Zoey said, shoulders back and rigid as she swung around to look at Johnny.

"Do you really have to swear so much?" he asked with a sigh. Beside me, Zoey flinched.

"What's your problem?" I asked, words sharp as I slid off my stool to stand in front of Zoey. Johnny looked down at me with an eyebrow raised, clearly not impressed.

"No problem, I just didn't expect Zoey to turn into a tramp like her friend." His eyes flashed to Roxie, an ugly smirk spreading across his face.

I took one step forward, not exactly sure what I wanted to do, but then Zoey stormed around me. Her eyes had cleared, sobering up in the face of her shitty ex, but the angry red on her cheeks worried me. Without thinking, I grabbed her arm, Olivia doing the same on Zoey's other side. Zoey pushed forward, flinging her legs towards Johnny. The man had just enough sense to step back before getting kicked in the balls.

"You're a fucking cheating asshole and you can't drive for shit!" she shouted, nearly swinging from Olivia's and my hold on her as she pushed forward.

"What would you know about driving? You're just a mechanic," Johnny scoffed, looking at his friends to back him up.

"I know I've replaced your brakes nearly every damn month since you started racing."

"We're racing on dirt, Zo. If you'd ever raced, you'd know you have to hit the brakes hard for a turn."

"I never raced because you told me *you* were worried about my fucking safety," Zoey screamed, arms thrashing. "I could race circles around your ass."

"I'd like to see you try," Johnny scoffed. "You barely drive as is. Bet you couldn't make it past the first turn."

"Fine. Name the date. I'll be there to kick your ass," Zoey said, leaning forward as far as our hold would let her. Johnny jerked back, some of that bravado falling. But his boys quickly nudged him back into place.

"End of February's open. Kinda unfair for you to go against, but I don't think anyone'll mind once they know you've gotta put a bitch in her place," one of Johnny's friends said.

Johnny didn't bat an eye at his friend calling Zoey a bitch. Like profanity only caught his attention when Zoey said it.

So I let her go.

And she immediately flung forward and shoved Johnny into his friends.

There were gasps and whistles as Johnny stood back up, nudging his friends aside. He stepped up to Zoey, who'd slipped out of Olivia's hold, and glared down at her.

"Fine. I'll race you. Maybe then you'll learn to be quiet."

Zoey opened her mouth to respond, but Johnny quickly turned on his heel to go.

But three steps away, he turned around, hand outstretched. "Birth certificate."

"Of course," Zoey said with a sickening sweet smile. I caught the glint in her eye, but before I could decipher it, she grabbed the paper and held it over the candle on our table. Small trails of smoke floated up from the center of the paper. Johnny pushed me aside, snatching the remains of his birth certificate from Zoey, and waving it around frantically to put out the remnants of flames.

"Fucking Christ, Zoey. Have you gone insane? I need this for my fucking job."

"You and I both know your mother has a copy," Zoey said, hands on her hips. "I'm sure once you explain the situation, tell her all about what you did, she'll give it to you. Or maybe not. Your mom always did like me."

8

SHOW ME HOW YOU USE THAT HAMMER

ZOEY

I was just like that fucker's birth certificate. Burning in the center, the fire eating away at me. Except I didn't have anyone to pull me away from the flames.

"Zoey, wait!"

I turned to see Stephen rush out of the Pub, my jacket in hand. Damn, I was so angry I didn't even notice the February chill. That never happens. I fucking hate the cold.

When Stephen caught up to me, he held out my jacket so I could slip my arms in, then zipped me up.

This little weirdo had shown me more kindness, more tenderness today than the man I loved for over ten years had in recent memory.

God, when would this burning fucking end?

"What can I do?" Stephen asked, hands still on the zipper at the base of my throat. I wrapped my hands around his wrists and guided him to my cheeks. So far the only thing that had dulled the burning was ...

"Did you like kissing me?"

Stephen sucked in a breath, his eyes falling to my lips.

"Yeah," he whispered. "Let's do more of that, then. When we get home. If you want."

"If I want?" Stephen's eyes shot to mine, wide and bright. Excited maybe. It was hard to believe he'd get excited over me. I was just some tomboy in overalls. I wouldn't say I had a lot of feminine charm, and what I did have was buried under several layers of baggy clothes.

"You can say no. I'm not gonna kick you out onto the street if you don't wanna make out or whatever." I let go of his wrist and stuffed my hands in my coat pockets, intending to walk back to the house so I could hide my embarrassment. But Stephen didn't move away when I let go. He stayed there, hands on my cheeks, keeping me in place.

"No, I definitely want to. I just …" He stroked my cheeks, his fingers cool against my skin. "You've sobered up, right?"

"Unfortunately," I answered with a laugh. Stephen kept looking at me, eyes bearing down, and when I tried to turn away, he held me still. He held me still and leaned in to rest his forehead on mine, our breath mingling, becoming one. Then his lips brushed mine. Tender, soft. Each touch was hesitant, like he was waiting for me to back away.

But soft and tender didn't soothe the ache. It highlighted it. It outlined every clue I ignored when it came to Johnny. I needed something *more*.

Without breaking the kiss, I pulled at Stephen's belt loops to maneuver him into the alley between shops and pushed him against the wall. He gasped and I deepened the kiss, even as I tensed in anticipation of him pushing me away. But he didn't. Stephen's fingers tangled into my hair, pulling me closer, tilting my head so that when he licked into me, something melted. Melted and gave way to a different heat, not the burning fire of anger, but a hearth.

I pushed into Stephen, pressing our bodies together, relishing in the comfort of kissing someone closer to my height. Everything matched up easier. There wasn't any straining or pushing to my tiptoes. We were even. Natural.

And things that I'd never done before felt natural too. Like letting the excitement drive my movements, even if they became sloppy. Like sliding my hands under his shirt to feel the warmth of his skin and *grab* it. Like dragging my teeth along his bottom lip, nipping as I pulled away.

"Fuck, Zoey," Stephen groaned and I froze, moving as far back as his hold let me.

With the lusty daze broken, embarrassment set in. I fucking bit this man, this stranger. All because ... it felt good and nothing else had felt that good in so long that I was desperate.

"Zoey," Stephen said, his fingers trailing down to my chin, refocusing me.

"Sorry, that was ..." Embarrassing? Stupid? Made my blood sizzle?

"That was hot as fuck," Stephen said with the sort of straightforwardness that made me laugh.

"Really?"

"Really," he repeated, pushing his hips forward so I could feel just how hot he found it. But before I could really appreciate it, he pulled back. "I just ... we should clear things up before we get back to your place."

"Like what?" Tomorrow I was starting a list of things Johnny stole from me. Like *learning how to date and fuck around as an adult*. I was turned on and floundering and just trying to push that asshole out of my head with my weirdo here.

"Um, well you said you want to kiss. Is that all you want?"

"I ... I don't know," was all I could get out. Because I did want more. But ... it'd only ever been Johnny. I only knew what it meant to fuck him. Everything else was ...

"That's okay. I'm ... *very* interested in having sex with you. But you're in control."

"Well, I do kinda have you pinned to a wall. In an alley. In a strange town."

"I'm enjoying it," Stephen said, a smile slowly lighting his face. It was cute, a little awkward, but cute.

Stephen's hands slid away from my face, one resting on my hip and the other moving behind him. He pulled out his phone, scrolling and tapping until he found whatever it was he needed, and turned the phone to me. The screen was filled with ... I don't know, medical shit.

"What am I looking at?"

"Oh. Um ... my last STD screening. Just in case you decide you want more than kissing."

"Oh." Fuck, this is the kinda shit I should've asked Roxie about. I let go of Stephen to dig out my own phone and pulled up my screening results. I held the phone out to him to see, heart beating in my ears. "Is that ... is that all you need?"

"Yeah, that's all I need," Stephen said after his eyes flicked to the screen then immediately went back to me. Then his eyes widened ever so slightly as he said, "And condoms."

"I've got condoms. So we're good on that front too." At some point, Roxie had snuck a couple of condoms into my pocket. Presumably, she sized Stephen up and gave me whatever she thought I'd need.

"Good. Let's go kiss. And maybe other stuff."

"And maybe other stuff," I repeated, nerves and excitement fluttering in my chest.

I forgot how good making out felt. The buzz, the butterflies, the labored breaths.

When we reached my house, Stephen spun me around and kissed me against the door. He was rough and needy. Just like I was in the alley. And I liked it, that trade-off. I liked the thought of being able to swing him around and take what I wanted and him doing the same to me. I liked the balance. The give and take.

With Johnny, I was only ever giving. Or maybe it was more accurate to say all Johnny wanted to do was take.

"Door," I mumbled into Stephen's lips, not willing to pull away but needing to get to the bed before the ugly, angry thoughts settled in.

Stephen grumbled something before grabbing my thighs and pulling them around his waist. I tightened my grip on him, digging through my pockets to pull out my keys. He slid the keys from my hands and unlocked the door. Inside, the door locked behind us, and keys dropped to the floor, Stephen carried me down the hall. His lips trailed hot kisses down my neck, nibbling at a spot on my collarbone that had me squirming, desperate for friction. I grinded into Stephen, relishing the way he stumbled in response.

Stephen was enjoying this, he was enjoying *me*.

Johnny didn't. He went out and found someone else to enjoy.

My back hit the bed and my head spun in 20 different directions.

Stephen was over me, hands braced near my head, knees rested on either side of mine. His eyes traced over my face, the speckles of green almost completely eaten up by his pupils. But all that hunger was still so soft. He took his time as he unzipped my coat, pulling me up by the waist to slide it off my arms and away. He took his time as he leaned in to kiss me, one patient hand on my waist. And he took his time whispering silly little praises. *You're so fucking cute. So gorgeous. You deserve more. Let me give it to you.*

All things Johnny never did or said.

"Stop," I said, voice rough as I put a hand on Stephen's chest. Without me having to push, he moved away, rolling to sit beside me on the bed. He didn't say anything, he didn't press, he didn't push. He sat there and waited.

Meanwhile, I stared at my ceiling willing the thoughts to *stop*. But there was too much to swallow.

"It's so god damn stupid, you know? That fucker *cheated* on me. For lord knows how long and with how many women. Meanwhile, I can barely enjoy kissing you without comparing everything you do to what he did. How he kissed me in high school, when he was in college, the last few years. How did he cheat on me like that? How did he not go mad with the comparisons? We ... we were each other's firsts and he's all I fucking know. How come he was able to fuck around while we were still together and I can't even do it after we're done? All I wanted was one lousy orgasm. Something that asshole couldn't give me for over a year now. And I can't even do that because of everything that fucker has done to me and —"

Stephen's hand found mine, warm and strong.

"You're right. It's not fair." He turned on his side, facing me, and pulled at my arm until I did the same.

"I'm just so angry all the time."

"You deserve to be angry."

"I just want to fucking come, is that so wrong?"

"No."

"That bastard owes me orgasms."

"I'd rather he not be the one to give them to you," Stephen said softly. I wiped away angry tears to see him clearly. His eyes were slowly regaining their color, but the heat of red didn't leave his face. "He doesn't deserve to see you come."

Words knotted together in my throat, tears burning at the corner of my eyes. All I could do was nod in response.

"What can I do to make this work for you?" His hand came up to stroke my cheek and I flinched away.

"It's the … the touching, the everything. It all feels different and I don't know what to do with different." I flipped onto my back so I didn't have to look at Stephen. "You should just go back to your room. Sorry for being a tease or whatever."

I could feel him looking at me, but when I didn't say anything, he got up. I kept my eyes focused on the ceiling, anger tightening my insides. I was so fucking horny and I had an outlet, a nice, slightly awkward, but knew-how-to-kiss-well outlet and I couldn't take it. I wanted —

"What if I didn't touch you?"

"What?" I don't know if it was the question or the way I shot up that made my blood rush. But either way, I was hanging onto his every word now. Stephen was standing in the doorway, leaning against the frame, eyes nearly pleading.

"What if I just … you know, talked to you. Told you what to touch and when. While I watch."

"I'm not very good at doing what I'm told," I remarked, nerves making me laugh.

"I think you'll enjoy it. But if you don't … I'll leave you alone to take care of yourself."

"… I kinda have a hard time with that too."

"What?" he asked and I just shrugged.

"I don't know. I've been with Johnny for so long, it feels … weird to do things on my own."

"Then how do you know what you like?"

Again, I shrugged. Stephen ran a hand through his hair, walking in a circle before he stood still in the doorway.

"Do you have any toys?"

"Kinda," I answered, scrunching up my face as I thought of the only sex toy I owned sitting in my bedside drawer. Charged, never used.

"What do you mean kind of?"

"It's ..." I crawled across my bed to pull the toy out. The hammer-shaped toy. "It was a joke gift from Roxie as a housewarming present. Johnny never wanted to use it or get any other toys, so it's all I've got."

"Don't say his name anymore," Stephen said, his jaw twitching and his hand on the door frame going white. He held out his other hand, palm up. "Toss it here."

I tossed the hammer to him, the dildo end landing in his open hand and rolling to the floor. Stephen murmured a curse, before picking it up and walking off.

"Where are you going?" I shouted after him, scooting to the edge of the bed.

"I'm washing this ... toy," he shouted back.

"It was only on the floor, for like a second."

"It's going inside you. I'm washing it."

"Wait what?"

Stephen returned, the toy shiny in his hands as he turned it around. I was frozen watching him examine it. There was so much care and thought as he pressed buttons, and ran his fingers over it. Each action made me wetter and hotter and just *fuck* I was finally going to get to orgasm. All because Stephen was able to come up with something that Johnny would never do. I didn't have anything to compare it to, so there was nothing to kill the thrill.

"All right, get those cute overalls off and whatever else you're comfortable with," Stephen said, tossing the toy onto the bed.

"You think my overalls are cute?" I asked, following his instructions and undoing the clips to wiggle out of the overalls. I tossed them towards the hamper and went to remove my sweater but my hands froze on the hem.

"You can do everything I'm gonna tell you to do just like that. You can even get under the covers if you'd prefer. But, yeah, you're overalls are cute."

"I was always told they made me look like a boy." I slid under the sheets even though my body was burning. It wasn't that I was particularly self-conscious about my body, but it was another thing only Johnny had seen, another thing to distract me. So to minimize the chances of distraction and maximize the chance of finally coming, I'd start under the covers.

"That's bullshit. Every time you raised your arms tonight, a bit of skin just above your waist would show. That's where my hands would go if you were sitting on my face."

I reached for the toy and nearly knocked it off the bed. "Sit where now?"

Stephen's eyes narrowed, grip becoming impossibly white on the door frame.

"Lay back and turn the toy on. Top button," he gritted out. His voice was rough, different from how he'd sounded when we were kissing or even when he'd first woken up. I couldn't do anything *but* what he said when he sounded like that.

"Good," Stephen said once I'd propped myself up on some pillows and brought the hammer to life. "Start by tracing your pussy through your underwear. Slowly. Linger over your clit."

I pulled the buzzing handle under the sheets and spread my legs to trace the tip over my cunt. Even on the lowest speed and through my panties, the buzz had me shaking. Especially when I dragged it over my clit, circling it a few times before moving on. Stephen's eyes never strayed from mine. Looking at him was ... escalating. Like he was stealing my breath and returning it with waves of heat and electricity.

"Are you not going to —"

"No," Stephen answered before I could get the question out. "I wanna stay focused on you."

"But you're ..." I trailed off as my eyes wandered down to the distinct bulge straining against his jeans.

"Don't make this any harder than this has to be, Zoey."

"It looks like you're already pretty hard," I scoffed. Though with the buzzing on my clit, the words came off way more strained than intended.

"Yeah, I'm hard as fuck. Why wouldn't I be?"

"Well ... you can't even see any of the good stuff."

"I can see your face. That's all I need."

My heart fluttered and I wanted to hate it, to cringe. But I couldn't. It was sweet and hot and it made every single one of my nerves stand on edge.

"But since I can't see, you've got to tell me, Zoey. How wet are you right now?"

"*So* fucking wet," I whimpered.

"Good girl. Now turn off the dildo."

"Wha?" I mumbled.

"That toy you've got is a three-in-one. I want you to play with the sucker before you fuck yourself."

"Sucker?" I repeated, reluctantly pulling the toy away and out from under the covers.

"At the head. See that little hole? You're gonna put that over you're clit and then press the second button. Okay? And make sure it's pressed up against you, like a vacuum seal."

"Vacuum seal? Is it gonna suck my clit off?" I asked, even as I slid the hammer back under the sheets and pulled my underwear aside to get the toy in place.

"No, it should feel good as long as you start slow. But if you don't like it, we can try the other side."

"What's the other side do?" My finger traced the second button, nerves battling the need to *feel*.

"The prong bit vibrates. So you can slide your clit in and pinch it to your comfort level. But go ahead and turn on the sucker. I wanna know if you like it."

I swallowed and pressed the button.

The buzz or vibration or sucking, whatever the fuck it was, had my hips lifting off the bed. It was so much *more* than I was expecting. It was just *good*. Good and warm and all I really had to do to keep that feeling was to hold a little piece of plastic against my clit.

Roxie should have told me how good this fucking felt. I would've done this ages ago.

"Zoey?"

My eyes fluttered open to look at Stephen. He was smiling, a crooked, excited smile that I wanted to kiss.

"How does your pussy feel, Zoey?"

"Empty." The word came out unbidden, but it was true. I kept clenching, expecting to feel a cock fill me. And when Stephen smirked in response, I seriously considered throwing a pillow at him. If I had this sucker on while being fucked, I don't think I'd be able to stop coming. And I very much wanted to experience that.

"We'll fix that in a second. But it's going to feel so much better if you come first. I promise."

I made some sort of unintelligible noise in response because with every pulse, my brain blended into mush. How come all Stephen had to do was look at me and say a few words to get me closer to coming than I'd been in months? If it was this easy, how come Johnny couldn't manage it?

"Do you like your nipples played with?" Stephen asked and when I nodded, said, "Then what're you waiting for? Show me how you like it."

I slid my free hand under my sweater, rolling a nipple between my fingers. Then I pinched and pulled and did whatever it took for the pulse of heat spreading through me to come faster, faster, faster.

My eyes didn't leave Stephen's. No matter how hard it was to keep them open and focused on the man in my doorway. I just couldn't look away. His intense watch sent a thrill through my body, nearly as strong as the sucker. And I liked that he was watching. That he was giving me exactly what I needed no matter the hoops he had to jump through to get there.

"That's it, Zoey. Take what you need. Take it."

"Stephen," I cried, pinching my nipple harder. Close, I was getting so close.

"Let me see you come. Please."

Incoherent nonsense fumbled out as my whole body seized. Pleasure damn near capsized me, drowned me. Everything was warm and it felt like I was melting into my bed. It was everything I needed. And when I turned the buzzing off, the noise didn't die, it moved through my body, my blood humming, reminding me what it felt like to orgasm. It was a good fucking feeling.

"That was …" I trailed off, words escaping me.

"Stunning. But you need more. Fill yourself up, Zoey." Stephen's voice was damn near gravel. His eyes were black with want. And I loved it, wanted more of it.

I kicked the covers away and Stephen's whole body went rigid. His eyes fixated on my cunt, mouth watering as I slid the toy inside me.

"Fuck," he hissed, turning in place and running his fingers through his hair. When he turned back to face me, his eyes flicked between my face and cunt, like he couldn't decide which he wanted to look at more. And when he finally spoke, one hand cupping his cock, stroking absent-mindedly, he said, "You look so fucking stunning, Zoey. Ravishing. I — fuck. Can you spread your legs just a bit more for me, pretty girl? Perfect. Fuck. Any man should be willing to die for this view, Zoey. You're perfect. Now turn it on and start fucking yourself. Please. It feels like my dick is gonna fall off if I don't get to see you come again."

"That sounds like an excuse a teenage boy would say to get his girl to fuck him," I said with a light laugh, even as I slid the toy out and then back in my cunt, shifting slightly until the tip could grind against my G-spot.

"No, I don't need to fuck you, Zoey, as much as I'd like to. I just need to see you come. Just one more time. Please."

I pressed the button the second he said please. There was so much I denied myself because of all the anger and heartbreak. But I couldn't deny Stephen. Not when he asked like he could barely breathe from all the want.

Keeping my legs open wide, I grinded the toy against my G-spot. Brushing it in rough desperate movements, pressing the button over and over until I found a buzzing pattern that matched the rhythm I imagined Stephen would use.

I'd known this man for a whole 24 hours and I didn't know if he had siblings, but I was certain of how he'd fuck me.

"God, you're so wet," Stephen whispered, voice full of wonder. His tone made me feel … a different kind of warm. It wasn't hot and horny, but comforting. Soft. Tender. The words, no matter what they really were, were a caress. The kind of caress there was no comparing to.

And that acknowledgment was the warmth that ushered my orgasm. Soft waves of electric heat passing through my body, slow and relaxing. Almost like getting into a hot shower, but better.

"How'd that feel, pretty girl?" Stephen asked. My eyes fluttered open, taking in the way Stephen was still standing in the doorway, still holding the frame, still hard as fuck.

"Really good," I answered, my voice uncharacteristically soft. I turned off the toy and pulled it out. I'd seen Johnny's cock after sex, but seeing my come on the vibrator was different. There seemed to be a lot more and I had no clue if that was a reflection of how good my orgasm was or what.

"Can I?" Stephen asked, holding out his hand but not moving. When I nodded, he stepped back into my room, taking the vibrator from my hands and ... putting it in his mouth. His eyes fluttered closed and he hummed around the handle. When he pulled it back out, it was licked cleaned.

"I'll go wash this for you. Then ... I'm taking a cold shower."

"You're not gonna —"

"No. I'm satisfied." Stephen stepped closer and leaned down to press a kiss on my forehead. "Good night, Zoey."

"Night, Stephen," I murmured as he walked away, head spinning as reality came into focus. Stephen was a man I barely knew, a *customer*, that was going to be stuck in town for a few weeks. Some of that stay would be in my house. And I just let him watch me jerk off.

Crap.

9

SURREPTITIOUS AND PECULIAR EXPLOITS BY AN ERRATIC DRIVER

STEPHEN

The first thing I did after waking up was check my pants. I wasn't certain if sexual stimuli before bed could cause a wet dream, but if it could, watching Zoey would definitely be a trigger. And that's to say nothing of the dreams I had about her and what we could do if that asshole wasn't so deeply rooted in her head.

Without letting myself dwell on why I was doing it, I created a very poor graphic that said, 'Johnny cheats for blowjobs' and rush-ordered some car magnets and stickers.

That done, I got up, got dressed, sat on the bed, and … tried to mentally prepare myself for seeing Zoey again. Because shit, what do I say? What we'd done last night was intimate and hot as fuck but there was no way it could continue.

Could it?

I did like Zoey. And obviously, I was attracted to her. And I'd proven I could make her come without touching her, so intimacy wouldn't be an issue even with the distance. Plus we have however long it takes for my part to come in to get to know each other properly. Despite the nonsensical beginning, things could work out.

As I reached for my phone to call Darren and ask what my chances were, a crash sounded from outside. I followed the noise, and the proceeding curses, out the house and back around to the garage. A *huge*, nearly industrial garage. While the outside matched the rustic small-town charm of Zoey's house, the dark metal garage door was pulled up to reveal something from a *Fast & Furious* movie. Or at least I thought so, I don't think I'd ever actually sat through any of the movies.

At the center of all the tool benches and car parts and lifts, was Zoey under a ... vintage car. A fast one, maybe. I really didn't know shit about cars. I wonder if that's something Zoey could teach me. I'd be interested to hear how many cars she's worked on, what —

"That lousy mother fucker," Zoey grumbled from under the car. She slid out, back on a little cart thing, and stopped right at my feet. Her eyes widened as she looked up at me, color heating her face. And then her eyes narrowed and all that warmth and emotion was gone.

"What're you doing out here?" she asked, sitting up to sift through a box of parts that sat beside the car.

"I heard a crash," I said slowly.

"Yeah, well the brake on this has been ridden down to fucking nothing, so I have to replace it before I leave."

"Leave? Where're you going?" This conversation was not going how I expected.

"Large auto shop up north."

"Oh." I guess that meant our time would be cut short. Maybe that's why she was being so cross. "Do they have the part you need for my car?"

Zoey turned to me, a look of sharpness I'd seen at the Pub last night. Mostly directed at Johnny. I was not a fan of it being directed at me.

"No. I told you, it's shipping from overseas. That's what you get for having a foreign car. I'm getting something for myself at this shop." And then she was back under the car, clanking and cursing every few seconds.

"So ... what about me?" It wasn't the right question, but one I needed to ask anyway. Because as badly as I'd like to talk about what happened last night, she clearly didn't. And I guess considering she was letting me stay here and fixing my car, I shouldn't push her for more.

"I'd start by calling the motel and seeing if they got a room for you yet."

"Seriously?" I asked and Zoey slid back out, jaw set.

"Yes. I don't want you hanging out at my house all alone." And back under the car she went. Without any further explanation.

I waited a few beats to see if she'd come back out to acknowledge the brusqueness, the turnaround from last night, or at least give me the name of the motel. But she didn't. She kept working on the car, occasionally singing along to the country twang of a fuzzy radio hidden somewhere in the garage. And I was left dumbfounded, questioning if yesterday really happened or if I'd dreamed it all. It wasn't outside of the realm of possibility that I hit my head and imagined everything.

I walked out of the garage with that possibility in mind, not really believing it but not knowing what else to think.

With nothing else to do, I pulled out my phone to figure out where I could stay tonight. But, along with some ignored messages from Darren, I'd also been added to a group chat with Zoey's friends. After introductions, they went through a series of threats for me to behave and encouragement for me to keep a close eye on Zoey.

Rosie: She's just not been herself since the break up and we're worried

Shea: And she's been extra crabby lately, damn near bit my head off when I asked if she wanted me to come over and hang out. I just thought she might be lonely in the house now

Roxie: You'd wanna bite someone's head off every time you're forced to remember somebody cheated on you too

Roxie: But I'm trusting you, Stephen, keep our girl out of jail at the very least

Unknown: I love and appreciate that y'all include me in every group chat, but I am so confused. Context please?

Olivia: We got a tad drunk last night at trivia with Zoey and her fake boyfriend and made a revenge list and now we're worried she'd gonna follow through

Bailey: I can't believe I'm missing * another * fake dating romcom (this is Bailey btw)

Rosie: I'm sure Zoey has enough sense to not do anything too bad

Shea: I dunno, some of the shit on that list was bat shit insane

Rosie: As long as she's got Stephen around, I think it'll be fine

Shea: Oh shit, Rosie is pro revenge antics *and* pro Stephen

Roxie: Me too, I think he suits her

Bailey: Oh man, that's high praise. Where do you normally live Stephen and will I see you in Snowfall for Christmas?

Me: I'm sorry to disappoint you all, but Zoey's no longer letting me stay with her and doesn't appear to want my company.

Roxie: Bullshit

Rosie: Oh dear, that's not a good sign

Ashley: I don't see what you all are so worried about. Getting a little revenge is healthy for her. Plus I'll get her out of any legal trouble

Shea: Very reassuring, Ash

Ashley: Well, I do feel bad for sparking the idea. I'll go check in on her after close

Olivia: Ooo do you have any cinnamon rolls left and can you save me some? I'll come over too. Maybe we can edit her revenge list some and make it a little less … illegal

Me: Zoey's actually leaving soon. Said she was going up north to some auto shop

Olivia: Excuse me?!?!

Rosie: She's leaving town?

Ashley: Is that really that weird? Seems pretty normal for Zoey to impulsively go to something car related

Olivia: She would've texted me if she was planning on going somewhere out of town

Olivia: Stephen, you have to go with! Lord knows what she could buy to fuck up Johnny's car

Shea: Oh shit, I didn't even think of that. Definitely go dude

Me: She doesn't seem to want to even talk to me, let alone go on a drive together.

Roxie: She's acting out because she's hurt, not because she actually wants you to leave

Roxie: But ignoring that, what do you want?

I shoved my phone in my pocket and turned back to the garage. Zoey was out from underneath the car and lowering the jack. When she caught sight of me, her hands went to her hips, thumbs resting in the loops of her tool belt. There was some grease or something on her forehead and her hair had been tied up.

It was a nice look.

"What? Need a ride to the motel or something? Give me a minute to grab my shit, then I can take you." She started to walk past me, but I stepped in the way.

"Fine. Grab your bags and let's go." She stormed past me and into the house. I followed her instructions without question. I went to my room, stuffing my few scattered belongings back into my bag then waited in the living room for Zoey, always looking over my shoulder in case she tried to sneak out without me. But she stumbled into the room, a small backpack over her shoulder and a tote bag hanging from her hand full of …

"Is that toilet paper?"

"Yeah, it's supposed to rain in a few hours." Then she was out the door again.

Had she been this confusing yesterday?

"Stephen! Let's go!"

I ran out after her, bag uncomfortably smacking my ass as I took the steps down from her deck. Zoey was waiting on the hood of the car, bags under her eyes. I opened my mouth to ask if she was okay, if she was bothered by me joining her, or if she wanted me to drive so she could sleep some more. But as soon as words started to form, she hopped off the car and got in.

I took that as my cue to get in and stay quiet.

So much for me offering to drive.

Zoey started the car, a slow smile spreading as the engine purred to life. I watched as she adjusted the mirrors, scooted her seat up, and readjusted everything. She seemed at peace in the car, like an angry cat calmed and cuddled up in a sunbeam. I still had several questions for Zoey, but it'd be nice to sit in this peace for a while.

But then she took off and peace couldn't exist at the speed she drove. In a neighborhood no less. Her neighborhood. And I would have told her to slow down, but there was no way she could hear me over the roaring of the engine or the squeal of the tires as she turned onto the main road.

Fortunately, the drive was short. Or the first part of the drive was short. She'd made it sound like we'd be on the road all day, but she'd parked the car outside a house no more than 10 minutes away.

"So ..." Zoey started after she killed the engine. She reached in the back for her tote bag, shirt rising just enough to expose the skin above her hip, the area that as soon as I saw it, made me realize I *needed* to hold her there. But then she settled back in the front seat and I pushed the desire away. "Did you mean what you said yesterday?"

I tried to run through a list of what I'd said yesterday. Most of the things that came to mind were from when I watched her masturbate. And I certainly meant every word I'd said then.

"Of course."

"Great. Let's start with this then." Zoey pulled a roll of toilet paper out from the bag and set it in my hands. Before I could even process what it meant, she was out of the car and chucking a roll of toilet paper towards the house.

Except she hadn't undone the first square, so the roll just flew over the roof.

"God damn it," Zoey murmured, reaching into the open driver's side to grab another roll.

"You've gotta pull some out first," I told her, holding out my roll and undoing five-ish squares.

"Oh, yeah, that makes a lot more sense. Well, show me whatcha got," she said, head cocking to the house behind her. I got out and rounded the car to stand beside her. For a second, I considered *not* TP-ing this man's house. Especially considering Zoey was doing this particular revenge activity because it was going to rain soon.

But then I looked back at Zoey, at the hope in her eyes that I wouldn't let her down like that fucker had. And there really wasn't a choice.

The roll left my hand, a trail of paper spiraling off as it went over the roof of the single-story home. When the paper settled, it created a stark white line down the black shingles, making it clear as day what we were doing.

I turned to Zoey, convinced she'd be as panicked as I was, that she'd want to bolt. But I was wrong. She was fully lit. Eyes sparkling, dimples showing as she giggled. She bounced in place as she pulled a long strand of paper free then tossed her roll over the other end of the house.

Now there were two stark white lines.

Three.

Four.

Now that Zoey knew what to do, she was throwing one after another. Laughing the whole time. Free.

I grabbed another roll and tossed it.

Zoey paused her TP-ing, looking over me with the widest grin I'd seen yet. She nudged me with her elbow before returning to our vandalism.

Well, Darren had told me to do something fun. I sure as hell got a lot of joy out of picturing Johnny's smug face falling when he saw this mess.

When I reached for the next roll, there was only one left and I held it out for Zoey. "Last one, make it memorable."

"Oh, I will," she said with a smirk. She took the roll and started pulling a long strand of paper free. I stepped back and watched, pulling my phone out just in time to snap a picture of her chucking the roll at Johnny's house. The roll landed right at the center, draping over the front door.

"Fuck that felt good," Zoey sighed. I stepped closer, wanting to take her hand, hug her, something. But then I remembered the looks she gave me less than an hour ago and I stayed where I was.

"All right," Zoey said with a clap. "Let's run!"

She took my arm, running me around the car and nearly shoving me in. Then she ran back to her side and jumped in, scrambling to start the car.

"What's the rush? No one's around," I said, looking over my shoulders to confirm there wasn't anyone watching our crime.

"No, but it's more fun to pretend like we're about to get caught, right?" And then she sped off like we'd committed the largest bank heist in Snowfall history. Her smile was just that valuable.

10

FUCK FEELINGS

ZOEY

The buzz of TP-ing your cheating ex's place, or at least the place he's staying, was exhilarating. It was like I'd chugged ten Monsters. It was more heart-pounding than my first car auction. It was …

"Do you have any siblings?"

I glared at the man in the passenger seat. I'd been trying, unsuccessfully, to ignore his presence and any memories his presence summoned. Last night was stupid. The things he made me feel, doing … whatever it was we did. It was all stupid and I didn't have the time for it. I had a race to focus on.

Plus he might be amused by my revenge plots now, but he'll get bored of me eventually. Or scared that I'll turn on him. I doubt he'll stick around for as long as it takes to fix his car.

And why was the first small talk shit he asked me the same thing I'd thought of asking last night?

"No, I'm an only child. Mom said I was too much of a handful to consider having more."

"I can picture that," Stephen said with a small grin. "I am too. Though I don't think I ever heard my mother complain about me like that."

"I wouldn't say she complained," I told him, clicking my tongue. "But I do think she wished she had a girly-girl."

"So you were closer to your dad?"

"You could say that," I scoffed because *lord* was that an understatement. I wouldn't go so far as to say my dad was my best friend, that'd make Olivia cry, but we were two peas in a pod. "He taught me damn near everything I know about cars. At least vintage cars. We'd be out in the garage nearly every night fixing something up."

"Was he a mechanic too?"

"Nah, a banker, actually. I never really thought it suited him, but it was a helluva lot easier getting my shop up and running since he had that financial experience. There was this asshole that owned the shop before me, the bastard barely met state standards for safety inspections. All the lifts and shit were rusted as fuck. And he still wanted to charge me a fuck ton to —" I stopped abruptly, realizing how easy it was to talk about shit with Stephen.

It used to be like that with Johnny, back in high school at least. But ... no, it was easy to talk to him about cars, about mechanics, shit like that. Other than my dad, he was the only one I could talk about that stuff with, so it was sort of *all* we talked about. Other things ... sometimes they were easy. Sometimes they weren't.

"Do your parents still live in Snowfall?"

I shook my head, hard. Trying to knock out all those thoughts.

"No. Mom moved to Tenseness after Dad passed to be with her sister and her kids."

"I'm sorry," Stephen whispered. I chanced a glance at him, ready to tell him off for any pity he might direct at me. But I didn't see pity in his eyes, I saw empathy, soft sorrow for me and my father, for what was lost. And even though I knew he meant well, that he was communicating that well, it made me uncomfortable.

I switched gears and sped up. Stephen noticeably shifted away from me, grabbing onto the ashtray on his door.

I guess I could be a little *nicer to him.*

"What about your parents? They live in Seattle?"

"Nah, I'm not local to Seattle or even Washington. My folks are from Ohio and still live there. I went to college in Washington, that's where I met Darren, and never left. I was never really close to my parents, so the distance hasn't mattered. Do you miss your mom?"

"Of course I do, but ..." I tightened my hands on the wheel.

"But what?" Stephen asked, voice lowered.

"But I understand why she had to leave. All those memories of them being together in Snowfall. Fuck, some days it's hard for me to just drive past the turn into their neighborhood. But I've got my friends here, my business ... Mom didn't have much left. Not enough to outweigh the pain of staying."

"When's the last time you visited each other?"

I let the question sit in the air, heavy. I was ashamed of the answer. If I didn't say it aloud though, the shame wouldn't be real.

"Why not?"

Fucker.

I shifted in my seat, words getting caught in my throat. I wish we were closer to the store or a rest stop for me to pull over and avoid this conversation.

"You don't have to —"

"No, it's fine. It's just ... I think we make each other sad. I remind her of Dad, she reminds me of Dad, and then we're just sad, depressed sacks of shit that can't talk to each other."

"I take umbrage with you calling yourself a sack of shit."

"Oh shut up, it's an analogy and you know it," I said, shoving his shoulder without taking my eyes off the road. "We just ... like with your parents, we didn't have much in common. Dad was what brought us together. And without him around, it's just hard. Makes us miss him more."

Quiet fell over the car, only interrupted as we crossed the line of radio coverage and the music faded to static. I left it alone because the static was *right*. It was how I felt, how my brain sounded. And as desperately as I wanted everything to just *calm the fuck down*, it wouldn't, *I* couldn't.

Stephen placed a warm hand on my leg, just above my knee, and squeezed. With his other hand, he turned down the volume. The static became softer and softer until it was completely gone.

"Where's he buried? We should visit tomorrow." Stephen stroked my knee with his thumb and I knew if I looked over at him, he'd have the most caring ass expression.

So I didn't look.

"He was cremated." I picked up his hand by the wrist and dropped it back in his lap. "We spread his ashes around the gazebo downtown. That's where he proposed to Mom, had their wedding, where she told him she was pregnant. All the big things. So ... we figured he'd like it there. In case any other big things happen."

I hated how easy it was to talk to Stephen about this shit.

And I hated that I was grateful for it.

But I was especially grateful when Stephen turned the radio back up, finding some music to fill in the silence of the rest of the drive.

11

——— ◆ ———

Obvious Needs Exasperated By Evading Discussion

Stephen

When Zoey said we were going to an auto shop, I assumed something like Auto Zone. A business with bright lights, shiny vinyl floors, and a clear floor plan with signs.

This store was pretty much the exact opposite of that.

For one, it was next door to a junkyard. There was no sign, no parking lot. And when we got inside, it was just a warehouse. Tall shelving units as far as the eye could see, not a label or sign in sight. Also not in sight, a cashier or any other employee.

And Zoey walked in like it was the most normal thing in the world.

"Zoey, are you sure we're supposed to be here? It doesn't look like —" I started only to be interrupted by an older, large gentleman who seemingly popped out of nowhere.

"That you, Zoey?" he asked, accent thicker than Zoey's. She turned to face the man, eyes lighting up.

"Bernie! I can't believe you're still running this place." She embraced the man like he was an old friend.

"Ah, they're not getting rid of me any time soon. I've got nothing else going on anyways." The two went on, catching up, exchanging stories on cars they've fixed up recently or how an idiot wrecked their vehicle. Thankfully I wasn't a subject for that latter part, so I could listen and nod along without having to add to the conversation. My preferred social interactions.

"So, Zoey, you looking for anything in particular or ya just browsing?" Bernie asked once the conversation slowed.

"Sorta. I've got a race coming up, dirt track, and I wanna charge something up real good. I've got a couple of cars that I think'll work, but I wanna see what y'all've got in stock before I decide. So I'm looking for intakes, exhausts, and forced inductions for any models ya got."

They went back and forth on the type of parts she would need, the different models she had, and all I got out of it was that Zoey knew more about cars than I did about programs. And she owned a lot of them. She listed off at least five cars she could work on and I was pretty sure none of them were the car we drove up in. I spent most of their talk Googling model after model. Most of them were from the 60s, one of which didn't even have a modern equivalent. But they all *looked* fast. They had those little wing things in the back and most of the models I saw had the racing stripes down the hood. That probably didn't affect their speed, but I assume folks didn't paint those on cars not meant for racing.

The best thing that came out of their conversation though was watching Zoey brighten. She spoke quickly, voice high in excitement, bouncing in place. Her hands were all over the place as she described her ideas for fixing up one car or another and how she wanted it to drive. She lit up the warehouse with her enthusiasm. And even though I barely understood what she was saying, I was smiling right along with her. There was something about her passion that breathed life back into her. It was enrapturing, beautiful. I wanted to keep watching her run around like a kid in a candy shop until I was sick of it.

But there was no getting sick of it.

By the time we were filling the car with Zoey's ten boxes of miscellaneous parts, the sun was starting to set. It'd taken us four, maybe five hours to get here. And since I couldn't drive a stick ...

"Are you sure you're good to drive back this late? I'd offer to take a turn, but —"

"Yeah, fuck no. No way am I letting you drive this car. No offense, but you wrecked the last car you drove and I'm not taking chances. I booked a room last night when I decided to come up."

"We're staying the night?" I asked, possibly shouted.

"Yeah, why'd you think I had you grab your shit?" she said, nudging my arm with her shoulder, clearly in a better mood than she had been this morning. "You'll have to grab your own room, but what're the chances you run into a fully booked place twice in one day?"

It turns out the odds were good. Or perhaps the odds were against me because I'd lied about the motel being full earlier.

When we reached the motel, Zoey checked in and immediately left me behind. So when I was told there were no rooms available, I had no choice but to trudge to Zoey's door to ask her to let me stay. Given her emotional shift from this morning, I was hopeful she wouldn't outright say no. We were both adults, we could share a hotel room without any awkwardness.

But when she opened the door and her face hardened, I knew it'd be a hard sell.

"What do you want?" she asked through the cracked door, the chain on. I could only see a bit of her face, but I could tell she was frowning, irritated. Like when she was talking about her parents earlier, especially her mom. Conflicted, that was the look.

Which was probably a bad sign for me staying in her room.

"There're no more rooms."

"Seriously?" Zoey scoffed. "God, you must have the worst fucking luck. Well, the next one's only a bit down the road. I suggest calling first."

And then she shut the door in my face.

"Seriously?" I gaped. "Can I really not stay with you?"

The door crept back open, the chain still on.

"Why can't you just call the other hotel?"

"And why can't I just stay here?"

"Because maybe I'm tired of seeing your stupid face and need some space."

"Stupid face?" I repeated, shocked that a clearly flippant insult stung so much.

"Ugh, fine, you have a cute face. But there's only one bed."

I waited for her to expand on that, to explain why it would be a problem. And when nothing came, all I could think to say was, "And?"

"And?" she practically shouted, shutting the door in my face only to fully open it seconds later. "It's *one bed*. We're practically strangers and I fucked yesterday up, I can't share a bed with you. God, how could you say and? Have you never seen a fucking romcom? Jeez. *And* my ass."

My instinct was to assure her that whatever she meant by fucking up yesterday, was untrue. Zoey gave me everything she could in that moment and it was beautiful.

But maybe she was avoiding the topic because she regretted showing me that vulnerability. Maybe all she wanted was a rebound and since that didn't work out, she wanted nothing more to do with me.

So for that reason, and that reason alone, I addressed another concern.

"Zoey, this is real life. We're not going to accidentally have sex because we sleep in the same bed."

"Shut up. I know that. I just … I'm not sharing a bed with you. End of discussion."

"But we haven't had a discussion," I tried to argue, but immediately stopped when Zoey crossed her arms and gave me a *look*. The look that said she'd like to see me argue my way out of this one. And I was not about to fight this woman who I knew, even after just 48 hours, was too stubborn for her own good.

"Okay, you're right. It's … awkward."

"Thank you," she said with an exaggerated sigh.

"But it's late and calling to get a room and getting a cab will take too much time. Can't I just sleep on the floor or something?"

Zoey sucked in a deep breath, her brow furrowed as she looked me up and down. Finally, she let out an exaggerated sigh and threw her arms up.

"Fine, whatever. Sleep on the floor. What do I care? I'll just let a stranger sleep in my close proximity, again. It's fine." She continued her grumbling as she walked into her room. I followed behind her, setting my bag on the desk and closing and locking the door behind me. I stood, facing the door for a second longer, willing the heart-gripping feeling to go away because I didn't even know what it was for. It was probably nerves. But what did I need to be nervous about? I was sleeping on the floor.

When I gave up on controlling the feeling, turned back to Zoey. She was seated on the bed, legs crossed, still grumbling. And when her eyes met mine, she scowled. "Stop looking at me like that."

"How am I looking at you?" I asked, trying my best to make my face as blank as possible, to hide whatever emotion was showing.

"Like your … I don't know, like I'm the bad one for not letting you sleep in bed with me. Like I —"

"You're not the bad one," I interrupted, stepping in front of her. "I just ... do I really feel like a stranger to you?"

It hadn't clicked until I said it, but that was the heart-gripping feeling, not nerves. Because despite knowing very little about Zoey and having known her for only two days, I felt like I *knew* her. And I didn't like the feeling not being mutual.

Zoey looked me in the eye, her blues so focused, narrowed in concentration. Then she threw herself back, crashing into the bed, wild strands of blonde everywhere. I very badly wanted to lay beside her, running my fingers through her hair. I wanted to lay there and get her talking like I did in the car. I wanted to hear about what crazy schemes she wanted to do next, if she liked what we'd done last night, and if I could get her number.

But I stayed still. Hoping she'd say something. Hoping she'd say the situation was embarrassing and she just didn't know what to do about it. Hoping that she'd say she wasn't ready for something after her breakup. Hoping she'd agree that we got along despite the short time.

She said none of that. For all I knew, she'd fallen asleep. It was time I resigned myself to an awkward car ride and an extended, lonely stay at the Snowfall Motel.

"I'll get ready for bed then," I murmured before grabbing my toiletries from my bag and closing myself in the bathroom.

I fell back into a routine that didn't change no matter where I was. I took my medication, flossed, mouth washed, brushed my teeth, washed my face, and put on lotion. It reminded me of a sci-fi movie, where to shut down the ship you had to flip each switches in order. And normally I was the ship, my routine winding me down so I could sleep.

But of course that didn't hold true tonight.

I left the bathroom having accepted that I wouldn't get any sleep.

In the main room, Zoey had changed into a large shirt and tucked herself into bed. At the foot of the bed, she'd made a makeshift sleeping bag out of the comforter and laid out two pillows for me. I looked at her to say thanks, but she was scrolling through her phone, the screen no more than two inches away from her face.

I took the hint and settled into my floor bed and the lights went off within seconds.

Eyes closed, I tried to fall asleep. But my mind decided it'd rather replay moments with Zoey. Touching her skin, kissing her forehead, watching her smile widen as she threw toilet paper at Johnny's house. The way she laughed with her friends, called me weird, screamed my name when she came. The sparkle in her eyes when she talked to Bernie about her projects. The fucking hammer toy and her taste.

"Are we really not going to talk about last night?" I asked, voice cracking halfway through the question.

There was silence for a long moment. So long I thought she might not have heard me or was already asleep.

But then a pillow landed on my face.

"Zoey," I grumbled, sitting up and tossing the pillow back in her direction. It was immediately chucked back at me. I tucked it under my arm and leaned against the bed. "Seriously, Zoey?"

From where I sat, all I could see of Zoey was a lump under the sheets. But then the sheets went flying at my face and she sat up.

"No," she grumbled. Her hair was all over her face, her arms crossed, eyes narrowed. It was becoming a classic look for her to give me.

"No, you don't want to talk about?"

"No, you don't feel like a stranger." She kicked at her sheets, sending them towards my face again. "You don't feel like a stranger and that's fucking ridiculous." She twisted around, laying on her stomach, facing me, her face just a few feet from mine. "It's ridiculous, right?"

"Maybe. But I don't really think so."

"Why not?" she asked, voice sharp, like I was crazy for thinking the whole situation ... wasn't crazy.

"I think sometimes people just ... match up. Especially when you let them see a vulnerable moment."

Zoey gave me a hard look, scanning my face for something. But then she smirked and said, "Are you talking about how I'm dealing with my break up or showing you my cunt last night?"

I snorted. Hard. Possibly sprayed spit but Zoey smiled in return. We laughed, soft and undignified. And when we settled, we each rested our head on the bed, facing each other.

"Either way, I appreciate you showing me both of those vulnerabilities," I said, keeping my voice low, doing my best to sound sincere, because I meant it.

Zoey shoved a piled clumped up sheets at my face.

"Did you serious just thank me for showing you my vagina? God, you're such a weirdo," she said through laughter. She gathered the sheets again, piling them into a makeshift pillow and resting her chin on it. "Is this how our friendship is always gonna go? You let me stew for a bit and then force me to talk about my feelings?"

Friendship. The word put a clarity to our relationship that I appreciated. And I very much preferred being her friend over being a stranger.

"Yeah, that'll be our thing."

Zoey's eyes widened, just a smidge before she shook her head.

"All right, friend, get in bed," she said, resituating herself.

"Seriously? You're okay with that?"

"God, yes, Stephen. It's too cold without the comforter anyways, so hurry up."

I scrambled up, scooping up the bedding and tossing it over the bed. Zoey tossed my pillows beside hers and we each took a corner of the comforter to pull it in to place. I paused by the bed for a moment, about to ask if Zoey was sure about this when I caught her glaring at me. I got into bed.

"God, you're such a weirdo," she murmured as I got settled under the covers. I laid down on my side, facing her and Zoey copied the movement. "All right, go ahead and say it."

"Say what?"

"Say that I was awkward and stupid last night and that you didn't like just watching and would rather I had just let you fuck me and you think I'm a stupid, angry girl for TP-ing my ex and —"

I put a finger to Zoey's lips. Her brow furrowed then she opened her mouth and, very gently, bit me.

"Zoey," I half grumbled, half shouted, pulling my hand away. "Why'd you do that?"

"I dunno, why'd you put your finger on my lips?"

"Because I wanted you to ... shut up."

"Rude," she murmured, nudging my leg with her foot under the covers.

"Dear lord, why're your feet so cold?" There was a swoosh of Zoey pulling her feet to the other side of the bed, then a mumbled sorry. I reached under the sheets, running my hand over her legs to pull her feet back towards me. Tucking them between my thighs, I said, "No, it's fine. Use me to warm up."

Zoey's face tilted down to where her feet were and she shook her head.

"Weirdo." I chose to ignore the comment.

"There were parts of last night that were awkward, sure. But not in a bad way. I enjoy spending time with you. And your friends. And I very much enjoyed kissing you. Would I have liked to have sex? Yes. But I would've regretted it if I found out you were uncomfortable or felt pressured or anything." Zoey rolled her eyes at that but I kept going before she could say something snarky. "And your anger ... you have a right to it. Your feelings aren't wrong or stupid or bad. And the TP-ing thing ... it made you smile.

I think the least that prick can do is take whatever you can throw at him if it gets to you to smile like that."

"You called him a prick," Zoey snorted, smiling softly. I wanted her to keep smiling. I needed it. It was like that moment when you take a sip of water and realize you'd been dying of thirst all day and needed to down a whole bottle immediately. That's what Zoey's smile was, the water I hadn't realized I needed.

"He is a prick. He also has a very punchable face." That made her laugh, deeply and with a snort.

"I slapped the shit out of him that night. Bastard has never looked more surprised." Her laughter teetered off, the sudden silence sharp and telling.

"I like you, Stephen. You're nice, you get my shit, I feel comfortable around you. And I guess you're nice to look at or whatever. But I ... I'm broken."

I pushed up on my elbow, ready to argue, but Zoey put a hand on my chest and pushed me back down.

"Don't get all up in fucking arms. I know I'm not *broken* broken. But I can't *not* be angry. It's like my gears won't shift out of it. You're sweet and kind and the exact right kind of guy and I'm pissed that Johnny wasn't. I'm pissed at myself for staying with him when I knew he wasn't everything I'd thought he'd be. You make me orgasm without fucking touching me and I'm pissed he had his dick inside me and couldn't even manage that. I'm so angry all the time and that just makes me angrier. It's a never-ending cycle. So that thing from last night ... it's just not feasible. *Nothing* feels feasible anymore."

Zoey shifted to lay on her back, staring at the ceiling, not blinking. It gave me the impression she was trying not to cry. And if it was anyone but Zoey, I'd have told her to cry, to let it out. But that wasn't Zoey. Or at least not the Zoey in this moment.

I took her hand in mine, squeezing twice.

"What *does* feel feasible?"

"Hmm, screaming, throwing shit, breaking shit. General destructive behavior, I guess." Zoey squeezed my hand once but kept her gaze on the ceiling.

"Then once we get back to Snowfall, I'll help you do as much *legal* destruction as possible."

"You really mean that, don't you?" Zoey turned to look at me, a hint of a smile pulling at her lips.

"I do. Not much else I can do until my car's fixed anyway. There're a few things I need to do for work, but I can do that during whatever your working hours are."

"Mmm, that gives my destruction a time limit. Gonna have to rush home tomorrow." She tossed my hand towards my chest and rolled onto her side, facing me. "I sleep on this side, so don't be a weirdo and turn over."

"Yeah, all right, Zoey. Good night." I turned over, shifting until I was comfortable in bed. Zoey's hand pressed to the center of my back, a light touch, and she whispered, "Good night, Stephen."

12

THEY CAN'T CALL THE COPS IF YOUR NAME IS ON
THE TITLE

ZOEY

When I woke up, snuggled against Stephen, warm and cozy, I was immediately pissed off. Because of course a damn near perfect man would show up in my life when I was too angry to enjoy it. I must have done some fucked up shit in my past life to deserve this sort of torment.

Whatever. I had bigger things to think about as we drove back to Snowfall. Namely how I was going to return this technically stolen car. I hadn't brought my phone with me, so I had no clue if Johnny had figured out I was the one who'd taken the GT or not. He might be a dumbass, dick bag, but he wasn't *that* dumb. The TP-ing probably tipped him off too.

But damn, I really did love this car. Johnny'd bought it right after he left for college as a thing for us to do together when he was home on break. I had so many memories around this car. Dad watching over us, trying not to be overbearing about his 'tips'. Making out on the hood. Hosing down the car and the each other on hot summer days.

It was bittersweet.

And he'd once again worn the brakes down to goddamn nothing.

"What're you thinking?" Stephen asked, tapping on the console between us.

"How do you know I'm thinking of anything?"

Stephen raised a single brow, a look I took to mean 'Are you fucking kidding me?' But then he tapped at his own furrowed brow. "The number of creases on your forehead."

Huh. Attentive little fucker, isn't he?

I drummed my fingers over the steering wheel, debating whether or not I should tell him about this car and its history. He might freak out about being in a partially stolen vehicle. He might try to get me to talk about my feelings more, which I surprisingly wouldn't hate, but I'd rather avoid it if I could. Or he could decided that TP-ing a guy's house was fine, but kind of stealing his car was crossing the line.

The nerves won over.

That and the idea of seeing Stephen's reaction when Johnny inevitably came over to reclaim his car was too good of an opportunity to pass up.

"I'll tell you when we get home. Just another ... 30-ish minutes. You can wait that long, right?"

"God, why does that make me nervous?" Stephen groaned, shifting back and forth in his seat.

"Oh don't be so dramatic. I'm not gonna make you hide a body or anything."

"Can you promise that will remain true for the foreseeable future?" I hummed, long and loud and dramatic. From the corner of my eye, I could see Stephen fighting back a grin. When he seemingly got that under control, he said, "I don't think Rosie or Olivia would approve."

One night out with my friends and Stephen could already make references to them.

"Well, Shea would help me hide a body, no questions asked. Ashley wouldn't, but that's only so she could defend me in court."

"You don't think you'd be able to get away with it?"

"Well given Johnny and I's history, if he goes missing, I'm probably the first one they'll bring in."

"Hmm, I guess I can be your alibi then."

"Oh, how sweet you," I teased, a hand to my heart. "We'll have to get our story straight beforehand though. Wouldn't want you saying we were eating pizza watching Gilmore Girls while I said we had Chinese and watched Supernatural."

"Then we can just say Jared Padalecki was on the screen before we got preoccupied with more important things. Pretty sure with a small town like Snowfall, they wouldn't ask any follow-up questions," Stephen said with a puff of breath that was almost a laugh. I'd just pulled up to a light that I knew from experience would take forever to change, so I took the opportunity to openly stare at the man next to me. When he caught me staring, he straightened up in his seat. "Sorry. I didn't mean to ... make you uncomfortable or anything."

"Nah, you're good. It'd be a good alibi. I just ... you're surprisingly smooth for somebody so weird."

"Me? Smooth?" Stephen asked, pointing to himself, which made me laugh.

"I know, I wouldn't've thought so either. But I think that's part of your charm, you know? It comes out of nowhere and sweeps you off your feet. Like ... damn, whatever it was you said when Johnny came by. Oh! Calling yourself mine. *Very* smooth. My heart may be on fire, but it still skipped a beat."

"Does that mean I get to stay with you instead of in a lonely motel room when we get back?" Stephen asked, cheek resting on the headrest to look at me. His eyes were soft, like a puppy dog, not begging because they knew they were gonna get what they wanted. Not in a spoiled way, just that they trusted their person. Stephen trusted me.

"Yeah, all right, I guess. But only for the alibi and pissing off Johnny. And your company isn't too bad either."

"So we'll still pretend to be a couple in public?" he asked and finally the light turned green, I could distract myself with the last few turns to home.

"Yeah. But we can tone it down if you're uncomfortable since the whole ... thing." I wish I could pull smooth moments out of my ass like Stephen.

"No, I think it's fine. As long as you don't mind that I'll still enjoy kissing you despite the fact that it's fake."

I nearly choked on nothing and crashed into a parked car. I side-eyed Stephen, half sure he was doing this on purpose. But he just sat there, fiddling with his fingers in his lap, eyes darting to me every few seconds.

"I guess that's a hazard of the job," I eventually grumbled, knowing damn well that I'll be enjoying whatever fake intimacy we share too. Whatever, I'll just consider it his payment for room and board. It's not like it was ever gonna be more anything more than that considering he'll be gone the minute his car's fixed.

It was real fucking stupid how my heart dipped at the thought of him leaving. All because he was nice company, a little weird sweetheart, and a hot kisser ... and watcher or whatever.

I might need to ask Roxie about voyeurism. That's the watching one, right? Or are there different words for being watched and doing the watching? And is it not voyeurism if it's not a stranger and in a private dwelling? No, that probably didn't count.

Maybe I should get into a kink, that sounds like fun.

"What's he doing here?" Stephen asked, the disgust in his voice so distinct and different from his usual tone, I jerked the car to a stop.

At my front door, sitting on the steps was Johnny. Blonde hair slicked back, jean jacket, and a glare that could kill. Good. He needed to feel as much anger as I did.

Without saying a word to Stephen, I parked the car at my curb, pushed the driver's seat back, and got out without turning the car off. Johnny wouldn't be sticking around long anyway.

"Fixed your breaks, dumbass. Try not to wear them down again so fast," I said without looking at Johnny, instead focusing on grabbing our bags and my boxes out from the back. Indifference. I was indifferent to his presence and the sight of him *didn't* make me want to scream and vomit. Fake it till you make it, right?

"You. Stole. My. Fucking. Car," Johnny said as he stood up, each word gritted out between bared teeth.

Stephen, who'd just stepped out of the car, folded back in, collapsing into a fit of laughter. My attempt at indifference was instantly blown away. I mean, who could help smiling when you've brought a man down like that? Plus Stephen had a stupid laugh, it was deep and then hit a high wheeze. It was cute. Especially since, even through all our emotional conversations, he usually kept a stoic, thoughtful face.

"Yeah, all right, laugh it up fucker. I should've called the cops the moment I realized it was gone."

"One. You should stop cursing, it's not really gentlemanly. Two, my name is on the title and the title is with all the other important documents you couldn't be bothered to really look for." I took the boxes of parts out one by one, setting them on the curb. Then with my bag slung over one shoulder and Stephen's over the other, I slammed the trunk closed and leaned against the bumper.

Johnny was seething. He knew I was right. And he fucking hated it. I used to avoid correcting him or pointing out shit he should've known because I loved him and I didn't want to make him feel less in any way. But in turn, he put me down as a woman who knew shit about cars to feed his ego.

It was his turn to feel like an idiot.

"Well, like I said, replaced your breaks, for you." I tapped the trunk and pushed away from the car. "If you need any other work done, you'll have to call the shop. I'd recommend new tires and a rotation. But you're welcome to get a second opinion. If you wanna use this one for the race, you should get that done soon though. Not everybody else keeps these kinds of tires in stock."

Stephen, done with his laughing fit, stepped up beside me, sliding our bags off my shoulders and onto his. His free hand slid around my waist and pulled me closer as we started to my house, stopping at the porch where Johnny still stood.

"Well, you've got your car back. So we're done here, right?" Stephen asked, head tilting to the still-running car. Johnny stared down at Stephen, fully trying to intimidate him with his height. Stephen was unaffected. He cocked a brow and asked Johnny, "Are you gonna go or what? Because I've got better things to be doing."

Stephen pinched at my hip playfully and I snorted at his implication. That and the way Johnny's eyes zeroed in on Stephen's hand and his face paled.

I would've stayed there forever watching Johnny's stupid face twist. But Stephen pulled me away, stepping around Johnny and leading us into the house. We stood by the closed door until we heard Johnny leave, staring at each other with blank expressions. But once we heard the engine roar and Johnny speed off, we doubled over with laughter.

"I can't believe you actually stole his car," Stephen said through wheezes. "When did you even manage that?"

"Ah, I've never been great at sleeping, would rather spend my time doing something better, you know? And that dumbass left so much of his shit here. Including all the spare keys. All I had to do was walk down to the storage unit." I dropped my shit on the floor and collapsed onto the couch.

Already the buzz of making Johnny feel like shit was wearing off and I was itching to do something else.

Stephen watched me for a minute, still standing by the door. His head was tilted, eyes soft. No judgment, just quiet thinking.

And then finally he said, "Think we could have a bonfire?"

13

SPARKS AND MERRIMENT OVERCOME A RESURGENCE OF ENGULFING SADNESS

STEPHEN

Me: Zoey and I are back and are having a bonfire tonight to burn Johnny's remaining shit. She'd like you all to come, ideally with ingredients for s'mores.

Roxie: Hmmmmm, that sounds very couple-y. Do you have something to tell us, Stephen?

Rosie: Oh hush Rox, let them be

Rosie: I'd love to come, but I'm the only one manning the front tonight

Roxie: You work too much, but I'll be there.

Shea: Me too!

Olivia: I'll grab a fire extinguisher and then be on my way.

Bailey: Oh man, I wanna go! Can you GrubHub or DoorDash or whatever in Snowfall yet? I can at least order y'all food

Shea: God, I wish. Delivery still sucks. Though I'd probably go broke if I could order Panera whenever I wanted

Roxie: Oh for sure, the number of times I'd order Rosie's pancakes is ungodly

Rosie: They're not *my* pancakes, they're my great-grandmother's recipe

Rosie: Also, Stephen, Ashley is normally in bed by now, so she likely won't respond/be able to come

Ashley: Burning a fuckers shit is worth breaking my sleep routine for, I'm in

Messages continued to pop up, but I shoved my phone into my back pocket so I could go back to helping Zoey. Once we'd figured out the logistics of creating a fire pit in her backyard, she'd gone around the house to gather things. The box she'd grabbed to do so was nearly half her size, which probably wasn't a good sign.

"Zoey?" I called down the hall. There was a pause, then a clatter, then a series of grumbled curses. I turned into her bedroom to see Zoey in the middle of a pile of ... everything. There were papers and clothes and books and just everything. "You all right there?"

"I'm contemplating burning the house down," she grumbled, kicking at a pile of clothes.

"That's not advisable." I scooped up the clothes she was kicking and dumped them in the garbage box. "It's a nice house, it's *your* house, so burning it would only be hurting you."

"Ugh, I hate it when you're right." Zoey started scooping everything off the floor and dumping it into the box, wiping her hands when she was done.

Once we cleared the floor, Zoey dragged the box from her room to the guest room. She opened the closet there, tossing whole boxes of papers and summer clothes and photo albums.

I took one of the albums out while Zoey continued her trashing tirade and started flipping through it. All the photos were from her high school years, pictures of her and all her friends, several photos of her and Johnny, and photos of her and her dad, mostly around a car. I looked at Zoey, her back turned as she pulled more shit out of the closet, and then back at the photos.

She'd regret burning these later.

Quietly, I removed all the pages from the binder-like albums and slid them under the bed.

"What are our feelings on burning tax documents?" Zoey asked, still facing the closet.

"If they're older than five years, I think it's fine."

Zoey sighed, loud and dramatic, but removed a stack of files before tossing the rest of the folder.

"All right, time to set some shit on fire."

The fire blazed each time something was tossed in It'd grown concerningly large after several notebooks went in, sketches of cars instantly eaten up by the flame. Olivia clutched at the extinguisher in her lap for dear life while the rest of us cheered Zoey on.

But once all the things Zoey deemed worthy of burning were ash, we all sat, watching the fire flicker as the girls reminisced about similar late nights during high school. The chatter was soft, the s'mores toasted, it was a good night.

Darren will be proud of me for not having touched my work laptop for so long. I didn't even check it when we'd gotten back. Spending time with Zoey was more important.

Zoey sat beside me, features soft as she zoned out, staring at the fire. I slipped my hand under hers and squeezed.

"You feeling better?"

Zoey bit at her lip, thinking.

"Yeah. I kinda wish I'd been more selective in what I'd burned though. There were probably some photos of Dad in those scrapbooks. I'm sure Mom has copies but —"

I squeezed her hand and she stopped talking.

"I pulled those aside for you. They're under the bed."

Zoey smirked, the 'I should have known' kind of smile, and rolled her eyes.

"You're so weird," she muttered under her breath. But then, with a squeeze of my hand, added, "Thank you."

14

STICKER TRUTHS AND PAPER LIES

ZOEY

Being a small town mechanic meant work was either insanely busy or insanely slow. There was no in-between.

Today was *fucking* busy. Some kid had stolen their parents' keys and tried to do donuts in their yard. That little joyride resulted in three wrecked cars, including the neighbor's. One guy brought his boyfriend's car in for a basic check-up for a surprise trip to Disney, which normally would've been fine, but the guy worked remote so the car hadn't been checked on in years. And to top it all off, Dan's kids were sick, so he couldn't come in and help.

A week ago, I would've been grateful to have all this shit to do. Fuck, I probably would've stayed in the shop all night to finish it all up. I wouldn't have to think about anything, I could just work and not feel.

But as I worked today, I kept thinking about the cute little dumbass stuck at my house.

I wasn't really worried about him being alone, he wasn't a puppy for fucks sake. But I was … curious. What did he do all day? Did I have enough food in the house for him to make lunch? Would he watch porn while I wasn't there? Can you get computer viruses on your WiFi or is that just a computer thing? Stephen said he was a programmer, so he probably knew how to avoid porn viruses.

Stop thinking about porn when you're about to go home to a sweet weirdo you're attracted to but can't fuck because you're emotionally stunted because of some asshole.

"Hey, Stephen! I'm home!" I shouted as soon as I stepped into my house. I figured announcing myself was the easiest way to avoid any awkward walk-ins. Though I do hope that Stephen would shut the bedroom door if he planned on jacking off.

"Oh, hi, I um ... I was hoping to have the table set before you got home," Stephen said, stepping out from the kitchen with his hands covered in oven mitts.

"Finish what?" I followed him into the kitchen to see a casserole dish of mac and cheese.

"I asked your friends what your favorite dish is. They like to talk a lot. I don't think my phone has stopped lighting up since I asked. And that was well over an hour ago."

"Yeah, they do that. It's nice though." I stepped closer to the mac, grabbing a fork from the drawer to take a bite. It was hot as fuck, but it was cheesy and gooey and so damn good. God, I loved mac and cheese. Like I wanted to fist-bump over it like a guy whose team just scored. "But why'd you make it?"

"You told me you were having a shit day. So I thought I could make your dinner. As a friend."

Mhmm. And do you make Darren food?" I asked through another bite. *Fuck this is good mac.* I suddenly wanted to keep Stephen as my housewife just so I could have this mac every day.

Stephen did a quick turn, putting the oven mitts in the drawer across from the oven. But I'd caught the blush coloring his cheeks. I wanted to see more of it.

"You should give me his number so I can brag about how you're better friends with me after only a few days," I teased.

"Oh, he'd hate that," Stephen groaned turning around to assess me, the blush gone. Bummer. "I've got something else for you too."

Stephen left the kitchen and by the time he returned with a box, I'd fixed myself a large bowl of mac and was sitting at the table. From the box, he pulled out plastic-wrapped stacks of …

I nearly died choking on a bite of mac and cheese because Stephen tilted the item to show a car magnet that read 'Johnny cheats for blowjobs' in red Comic Sans with little stars around it. It was stupidly bad and the best thing I'd ever seen.

"Oh my God, Stephen, this is fucking brilliant!" I almost dropped my bowl on the floor trying to set it down quickly and get a better look at the magnets. I spun them around in my hands, giddy like a kid on Christmas.

"I got some stickers too, in case you want to start tagging Snowfall." Stephen pulled another plastic-wrapped stack out of the box and held up a sticker with the same design, only slightly smaller. I hopped out of my seat, gabbing Stephen's arm as I bounced around.

"Let's go, let's go, let's go," I chanted, shaking him in excitement.

"But what about the food?"

"We can reheat it. Let's go!" I scooped up the box and started to the door, Stephen grumbling behind me as he followed.

On my front lawn, I dropped the box and started tearing off the plastic. I stuffed a handful of magnets in one pocket and stickers in the other and handed stacks of each to Stephen.

"You tag that side, I tag this side?" I said, pointing across the street. "Well walk up to downtown then over to the Paper."

Stephen's brow furrowed as he stared at the stacks in my hand. Eventually, he took the stacks, staring at them for another long moment before looking at me.

"Two follow-up questions."

"Shoot."

"I thought you wanted to cover Johnny's car in magnets."

"Well, I'm excited and I wanna use 'em right away. Plus won't it be extra funny that he'll have to see the truth everywhere he turns?"

"Good point," Stephen said with a nod. "Second question, what's the paper?"

"Oh right, you've still got a lot to learn about Snowfall."

"It's the newspaper? The newspaper is called The Paper?" Stephen asked with the usual amount of disbelief most out-of-towners had when they learned about the naming convention for the older town establishments.

"Yeah. What else would you call it?" It was well after closing, so the few office buildings in Snowfall were dark. *But* Olivia had once told me they kept a spare key in one of the potted plants out front, so it was only a matter of trial and error.

First pot, no luck.

"Why not the Snowfall Gazette? That sounds nice, quaint." Stephen was looking up at the sign over the door, adorably baffled.

"That's pretty long though. The Paper is short and sweet and to the point." No luck in pot two either.

"But it's just so ... wait, what are we even doing at the newspaper after hours?"

"Bingo!" I pulled out a key from the third pot and held it up like that one video game dude. Wiping it off on my pants and going to the door,

I explained, "Olivia used to work here. Twice, actually. But back in high school, she dumped coffee all over the editor's desk when he said some dumb shit and she lost her internship. Anyways, she told me about the key and what system they use to format shit. So we …" I paused dramatically, pushing open the door. "Are gonna add an article shit-talking Johnny before it goes to the printer tomorrow morning."

Stephen stared at the open door and when he hesitated for too long, I got behind him and pushed him in. "Come on, we can't get caught."

"Okay. So you are aware that this is a crime and you still want to do it?"

"Oh come on, this is nothing. I mean, it's not breaking and entering if we have a key." Once I'd pushed Stephen past the doorway, I shut and locked the door behind us.

The office was oppressively dark, not even the dull glow of a computer screen to light our way. All I could see from the streetlights outside were the shadowed outlines of desks. I remember coming to visit Olivia when she was interning here and I'd thought the place was huge, bustling. But now … it was practically empty. And I couldn't tell if that was a reflection of me growing up or the town … not growing. I couldn't remember exactly, but I'm pretty sure the Paper used to have more than three folks on staff back when I was in school.

"All right," Stephen said after a deep breath. "What're we doing and where?"

I smirked, happy I hadn't scared him off. Yet.

Lighting up my phone, I led the way to the back of the office and sat at McKree's desk. The lead editor had little going on in the way of organization, but he did have a sticky note of all his passwords stuck to his laptop. Bless old folks and their inability to remember one password with one or two variables.

That said, it did take me a couple of tries to get in and open up the right program. Once I had, I deleted a front-page article on the community garden opening up and replaced it with …

"Huh."

"Huh?" Stephen repeated with an edge of panic.

"Writing an article about Johnny getting cancer is harder than I thought."

"Cancer?" Stephen shouted. "You can't just tell people he has cancer, Zoey."

"Why not? He'll get a bunch of casseroles and be super annoyed about it."

"Casseroles? What? No. No cancer. And just a reminder, no saying he's gay or has STDs either."

"Ugh, I didn't mean anything by it, I just think he doesn't deserve sex and would like to decrease his chances," I grumbled, refocusing on the now blank space of the front page. "Is it still a no on the small dick thing?"

"I don't think —"

A clatter of keys at the front door made us freeze. Stephen took me by the arm and dragged me down onto the floor. Then he crawled under the desk and pulled me under with him. I'd just settled onto his lap when the door opened.

"Ugh, now where did I …" a soft voice came from by the front desk area, followed by the lights flickering on.

"It's just Midge," I whispered looking up to see Stephen shake his head.

"I don't know who that is, but I think anybody would call the cops if they find two strangers in their office at night." Stephen pulled me closer, nestling me between his legs and holding us tightly in place under the desk.

"I just meant, she'll probably be in and out. She does HR or something, so she won't need to —"

"Ugh, that man is always forgetting to turn off his computer," Midge grumbled, voice coming closer.

"I clearly said no schemes that would end with us in jail," Stephen grumbled, resituating us to ensure we were *fully* under the desk.

He was so nervous and fiddly, I couldn't help but fuck with him. So when Midge was just a few feet away, I stuck my foot out from under the desk, mostly blocked from view by the swivel chair. Stephen caught it, gripping my thigh and dragging my leg back out of sight.

"Now is not the time for you to be naughty, Zoey," Stephen growled into my ear, soft and rough and very intriguing. Fucking with him was *fun*.

"When is the time to be naughty?" I asked, half breathy, half giggling.

"God, it's like you enjoy torturing me, pretty girl. It's not nice. I want to kiss you so fucking badly and you know it," he grumbled. His legs shifted up and his arms wrapped tightly around me so that I was essentially locked in his embrace. His head dipped, nuzzling into my neck, lips brushing over sensitive skin. I leaned into him, into his touch. His lips grazed across my skin in one deliciously slow pass. Then he dipped back down, his tongue joining the fun. I squirmed against him, biting back a whimper, and Stephen held me tighter. His grip tightened before his teeth began to sink into my neck. And ...

"Mr. McKree could at least turn the monitor off before leaving," Midge said from somewhere above us. There was a click and then the light from the monitor went off.

We sat under the desk, frozen, as we listened to Midge walk out of the office and lock the door behind her. Then we sat for a second longer, Stephen's lips still resting on my neck.

Then sense kicked in and I scrambled the fuck away.

"Squirrels," I muttered when Stephen joined me out from under the desk. He looked around the floor, face furrowed. "Johnny's afraid of squirrels. One bit him or something when he was little and he freaks the fuck out whenever he sees one. Caused a crash once."

"Oh." Stephen straightened, but his hands twitched at his side. "That's good, write about that then. I'm sure he has shitty friends that would make fun of him for it."

"Yeah," I said softly, sitting back at the desk to turn the monitor on and write something as quickly as possible. "He wouldn't even let me have a cat because of it. Said their tails creeped him out."

"You should get a cat then," Stephen grumbled, turning to rest his ass on the desk as he watched me type. I expected him to say more, to caution me about writing anything too mean, but he kept quiet. So I did too.

15

WHEREWITHAL TO ABSTAIN TRAMPLED BY CUTE HOST

STEPHEN

Zoey was gone before I woke up the next morning. Which wasn't surprising since I was pretty damn close to giving her a hickey under a desk last night. No wonder she didn't want to see my face.

At least she texted me before she went. Just a simple 'heading to work early' but that's better than a cold nothing.

I sat down at the kitchen table with my computer open, willing myself to focus on the code in front of me. Focusing was the one thing I was good at. Dennis claimed it was a double-edged sword because I had a tendency to do nothing else *but* work when I was focused. But I could use that sort of concentration now, surrounded by reminders of Zoey and how cute and lively and fucking sexy she was.

There was something about the switch from her being crass and angry to teasing and flirting. It flipped a switch inside me. She flipped so many fucking switches inside me, I was going to short circuit soon.

I leaned my head back, staring at the ceiling, and stuck my hand in my pants to scratch under my balls because fuck it, I was alone. I'd be alone for several more hours. I could do whatever I wanted. Even ...

"Hey, Stephen! Somebody put a bunch of stuffed squirrels in front of Johnny's ..." Zoey stopped speaking after she'd tossed her keys on the table by the door and turned to see me, sitting at her dining room table, with a hand in my pants.

"We're you gonna ..." She made a jerk-off motion with her hand, then gestured at the dining room, clearly fighting a smile. "In the dining room? That was never an option in the versions of Clue I played."

I shot out of my seat, hand *out* of my pants.

"No, I wasn't."

"You weren't?" she asked, an eyebrow up in disbelief. I sat back down and buried my face in my hands.

"I wasn't. I was just considering ... doing it. Elsewhere. Maybe. I hadn't decided. I really should be working."

"Huh," was all Zoey said before walking over to the dining room, pulling out a chair, and sitting in full view of me. "Can I watch?"

"Wha?" I had to be dreaming. Zoey had made it clear she wasn't in a space to do anything else and this felt like *something else.*

"You watched me, so it's only fair." She moved around in her seat, getting comfortable for a show I guess.

"Here?"

"I mean, that's what you were gonna do anyways, right?" She nodded to my crotch and I could feel every molecule in my being burn.

"I really *wasn't* going to do it here."

"Why not? The hardwood is probably easier to clean up than a sock. And you can sit down, unlike in the shower."

"Zoey, are you asking me to come on your floor?"

"No. I'm asking you to *watch* while you jack off. I don't particularly care where you come, so long as you clean it up," she said with a shrug.

"So if I wanted to come all over your face, would you let me?"

Zoey's eyes widened and I opened my mouth to apologize. But then she slid off the chair and onto her knees, crawling to kneel at my feet.

"As long as you clean it up," she repeated, her voice breathy, eyes darkening.

"Christ, you really are trouble, aren't you, pretty girl?" I waited a beat for her to pull away, say she wasn't ready or interested. But she didn't move. She stayed in place, looking up at me with those big blue eyes that were getting darker and darker by the second.

"We're really doing this, huh?" Zoey nodded, licking her lips as her eyes dropped to my crotch. The look had an effect.

I ran a hand through my hair, trying to think this through.

"All right, but I … it's not gonna be a long show, Zoey. And I might grab your hair to move you so I don't get any in your eyes or hair. That all all right?" She nodded, scooting just an inch closer, killing me with every movement. Did she know what she was doing to me and didn't care or was she completely unaware and focused on my straining cock?

"And you're still in control. I so much as get my pants a centimeter down and you're uncomfortable, we stop. I get halfway there and you decide you don't like it, we stop. I'm in the middle of coming and you don't like the smell or it being on your face, we —"

Oh my god, Stephen. This is all good and healthy, but just take out your cock," Zoey said, huffing the last word like maybe I was killing her a little too.

Something between a sigh and a groan passed my lips as I pushed my pants down and pulled out my cock. I started stroking myself, fighting to keep the motion slow as I watched Zoey's mouth drop.

"Oh."

"Oh?" I repeated, but I could see it in her eyes, the desire, the want.

"You're … well you told me not to make fun of smaller men. You definitely weren't saying that because of some secret insecurity."

"I can't say I hate the way you're stroking my ego," I chuckled. Zoey's eyes met mine, bright with a smile that could melt my fucking soul. And then she looked down at my cock, focusing on how my hand moved, and a whole other part of me burned.

"Go faster," she whispered.

I went faster.

Every single piece of this moment would be forever engraved into my mind. And she wasn't even touching me. But I *felt* her. I felt the way her eyes lingered over my movements, felt the way her breath caught in her chest, felt her when her eyes flickered up to mine to check in. It made my body buzz.

My motions slowed, not ready for this moment to be over. Because after this, then what? Things get awkward again until she needs me to play a part or help her exact revenge. And as much as I was enjoying those moments, I just wanted this one to live a little longer. That wasn't selfish of me, was it?

"Keep going," Zoey whined, a hand clutching at my pants, pinching my skin just enough for me to *feel* it.

I jerked up, standing. The hand around my cock stroked with new fervor while my free hand went into Zoey's hair, twisting into her light strands to angle her face. She moved willingly, pushing up onto her knees so that she was closer. Almost too close. Because the way she parted her lips, licked them, gave me a clear vision of what else we could be doing. Of how it would feel to glide in and out of that snarky mouth of hers. Of how she'd listen when I told her to take care of herself while treating me.

"Fuck, I'm going to come, pretty girl." My grip tightened in her hair and I waited for her eyes to close or her lips to press into a tight line.

But she stayed just as she was, watching, lips slightly parted. A vision. A vision that caused me to combust.

Strands of come landed across her cheek and parted lips and caveman-like satisfaction washed over me. And it was made worse when Zoey licked her lips clean.

Stuffing my cock back in my pants, I snatched some napkins from the table and sunk to my knees.

"You shouldn't have done that," I murmured as I gently wiped my come off her face.

"Why not? You got to taste me?"

How many more times can she kill me with want?

"I did. And you were delicious. But ..." I folded the napkin and set it on the table before sliding my hands over her cheeks, behind her neck. "But I promised to clean up. And now I can't do that without kissing you."

I felt her swallow under my hand but when she spoke, her voice didn't show a hint of nerves. "Then kiss me then."

I pulled back to get a good look at her. Zoey's eyes were hard, stubborn. But she was biting her lip.

"No, I don't think I will." I saw Zoey's face start to drop, but before she could pull away, I stood and scooped her up.

"Wait, what're you doing?" she squabbled, squirming in my hold.

"I like you, Zoey. And I want to treat you right." She stilled.

"Okay?" She said the word hesitantly like she wasn't sure if she wanted me to expand on that or not.

Silently, I took us into the bathroom and set her on the counter. I turned on the sink and waited for the water to warm. Once it was warm enough, I wet a wash cloth and started wiping Zoey's face.

"So you're just not gonna say anything after that?" she asked, crossing her arms and narrowing her eyes.

"I was letting you think," I murmured, focusing on her soft skin and the flakes of dried come on her cheek. "Remember? You get to stew a bit and then we talk."

Her scowl dropped and she fought a smile, rolling her eyes at me, shoulders relaxing.

"I already told you I liked you. We don't need to pussyfoot around it."

"Pussyfoot?" I repeated, barely holding back a laugh.

"You know, pussyfooting, like beating around the bush."

"Ah, I know that one." I dapped the washcloth against her nose, making her roll her eyes at me again. "So I like you and you like me. And we've enjoyed watching each other get off. But you're nervous and not emotionally ready for anything."

"Who said I was nervous?" She started biting at her bottom lip again, so I set the washcloth aside to take hold of her chin and pull her lip with my thumb. Realizing what she was doing and that I'd noticed, she pouted. "Whatever, it's normal to be nervous."

"It is." I let go of her face and reached around Zoey to get a bit of my face wash. Then as I spread the soap over her skin, I continued, "But I think part of your nerves are tied to being in that stage of anger. And I don't want to rush you past that."

"But you're leaving once your car's fixed," Zoey said, voice quiet, eyes dropping. I tugged at her chin to bring her face back up.

"We have phones, Zoey." That got me another eye roll and a light shove.

"Sure. But I've seen you ignore at least seven calls from Darren so far."

"I wouldn't ignore your calls. Darren just ... talks *so* much," I sighed.

"I know the feeling," she said, snorting. I was going to fall in love with that laugh. "Olivia gets on my ass all the time about not responding in our group chats. But I swear, there's like 20 of them and sometimes I just don't have shit to say. It feels dumb to just thumbs up emoji to everything just so they know I read it."

"Exactly. But ..." I paused to grab the washcloth and rinse her face. "I like talking to you. So if you call, I'd pick up."

"So you're willing to make a long-distance relationship work."

I finished cleaning Zoey's face and rested my forehead against hers, eyes closed.

"I'm willing to make long-distance work," I repeated, even as images of regular trivia nights with her friends, late night binge sessions curled up on her couch with a cat came to mind. "And I'm willing to wait and help you heal."

Zoey's hands found mine, entangling our fingers together. She squeezed twice and I returned the gesture.

"What if the anger never goes away?" Her voice was quiet, like a slow knife sinking into my gut.

"Then we deal with that together. I can't promise you forever yet. But I can promise I'll do everything in my power to make you feel better." I pressed a soft kiss to her cheek, pretending I didn't notice the tear there.

16

MIDNIGHT QUESTIONS

ZOEY

"Roxie, are you busy?" I asked as soon as she picked up the phone. I felt a little guilty calling her instead of Olivia. But seeing as Olivia never really got over her first, albeit fake, boyfriend, I figured I could use advice from somebody who had more experience dating around.

"For you, never. What's up?"

Nerves popped the words before I could get them out. So I pivoted to something else.

"What do you know about voyeurism?"

"Pretty wild topic to start a call past midnight with. Why do you ask? Were you peeping on your hot guest?"

"It wasn't *peeping*. I was sitting right in front of him."

"Zoey! Shut up!" Roxie screeched. I heard a bunch of shuffling like she was sitting up in bed as the call got more interesting. "Tell me everything! From the top. I wanna know the lead-up."

"Oh ... well you see ... god, is it always awkward to describe sex like this?" I found myself shuffling on my bed, for an entirely different reason. Roxie talked about her sexcapades with us. Lots. The other girls did too. Shea taught us a *lot* about strap-ons. But I never felt like I had much to add. With Johnny, it was always same old, same old.

"I mean, it could get easier the more you do it. Or if you don't wanna, you don't have to. I'm just excited for you. Was it good?"

"The watching? It was ... hot. Does that mean I'm a voyeur?"

"I mean, kinda. But all kinks have levels to them. Watching a partner masturbate or mutual masturbation is a pretty common interest. It's also good for new partners in terms of getting comfortable with each other and learning what the other likes."

"What he likes?" I was paying *very* close attention to everything he'd been doing, but I'm not sure I adsorbed any usable information. I was mostly just thinking about how big he was and how wet I'd gotten watching.

"Yeah, like tempo, grip tightness, if he likes playing with his head. When you're with somebody, especially the first time, it's kinda awkward to be like, 'No direct pressure on my clit, please'. But if you watch somebody, they'll do what they prefer naturally and you can copy that."

"Oh. That makes a lot of sense. I should've ... I dunno, took notes or something."

"I'm sure you picked up more than you thought. So ... you and Stephen, huh? How's that going?"

Right. The real reason I called.

"It's going ... not great."

"Oh my god, do I need to beat his ass? Shea should be closer, I'll call her and —"

"No! God, why do y'all always jump to needing to beat someone up?"

"I dunno. Might be a Southern thing."

"Oh, is pussyfooting a Southern thing too? Stephen seemed confused when I said it."

"Maybe?"

"Whatever. Doesn't matter. *I'm* the problem here." She made a sound of dissent, but I kept talking. "No, I am the problem. I like him, he likes me, and we oddly just sorta click. I'm mildly convinced Clive is working for Cupid. That's the only logical reason for this near-perfect man to wind up in my shop. But I just *can't* do anything about it because I'm still not over Johnny."

There was a long pause before Roxie asked, quietly, "Do you want him back, honey?"

"Ew. God no." My response was automatic and without a single ounce of doubt. Since I saw him in the hospital room, there hadn't been a second I wanted him back. I'd known our relationship was failing, I could feel it but wasn't ready to admit it. And him not even trying to deny it or explain himself certainly helped rip the band-aid off. "I'm not over him in the sense that he lives rent-free in my head. Always in the back of my mind, pissing me off. How do I get over *that* part? You've been with a lot of guys, *surely* one of them got stuck in your head. How do you get over that?"

"Well, honey," she started with a sigh. "Normally, I'm all about getting under someone new. Sex is fun and fun can help you heal. Plus it's a good reminder that you can still *feel* outside that last relationship, that somebody else can make you feel just as good or better or as much."

"I never thought about it like that. Fuck, you're so fucking insightful when it comes to this shit," I said, in complete wonderment over my friend. Why had I never been able to see sex this way?

"I am a wonder," Roxie said, a smile in her voice. "But I don't think that line of thinking is gonna help you. You gave a lot of yourself to Johnny and he still has it. You need to find a way to take it back. The problem is, there's not any one way to do that. And only you can figure out which is the right way for you."

"Very helpful," I scoffed, even though I knew she was right. But what could I *take back* from Johnny? Everything left was sort of intangible. Except ...

"Oh, I've got an idea. Talk to you later."

"All right, stay safe, don't go too far off the deep end. Love you," Roxie said with a kiss noise.

"Love you too, Rox. And thanks. I ... I like the way you talk about sex."

"Why thank you. Next session, I'll have to charge you."

"Oh fuck off. When's the last time you paid for an oil change?"

"Touche, touche."

We said our good nights, then I hung up and let my phone fall onto the bed. I considered not waking Stephen up in the middle of the night to join me on a borderline illegal revenge scheme. I mean, if I really wanted to, I could get everything done by myself. But I liked bringing Stephen along. I liked how he complained and still went along with it. Liked how even though he did complain, his complaints never felt like criticism of me.

Not giving myself a chance to linger on that, I scrambled out of bed, tiptoed into Stephen's room without knocking, and hopped onto him. Stephen jerked up, one arm damn near smacking me in the face.

"Zoey?" he grumbled, looping an arm around my waist and pulling me down onto the bed. "You don't have to literally jump to jump my bones."

"Stephen, I'm not here to jump your bones." It was hard not to giggle at his use of 'jump my bones'. In fact, I didn't even try, especially since Stephen started tickling my sides as he pulled me closer.

"Don't lie, pretty girl." He pressed a kiss to the back of my neck, probably getting a mouthful of hair. "I need you too."

The words burned. They burned in a different way than my anger and I couldn't identify why. But I knew I couldn't hear any more of that kind of talk.

I turned over and shook Stephen fully awake. His eyes fluttered until the hazel color sharpened.

"Zoey?" he asked, voice clearer too.

"I need your help with something. Let's go."

17

Leverage Over Offenders Keeps Officers from Undermining Taunts

Stephen

I don't think I really understood what was happening until Zoey parked in front of Johnny's house again. Without a word, Zoey got out and went to her trunk, where she pulled out a tool bag. Then she walked around the back side of the house, disappearing from sight.

I sat in the car, waiting for my memory to click into place. It wasn't outside the realm of possibility that she told me what to do when she first woke me up and I'd forgotten. I'd never done well with being woken up suddenly. Darren likes to tell this story where, during our freshman year, he came back trashed and got our beds switched up. When he tried to crawl into bed, I'd socked him in the face.

But I'm pretty sure she hadn't told me to wait in the car.

After a solid minute, I followed after Zoey, trying to be as quiet as possible. Rounding the house, I found her in the backyard. Under a car.

"Zoey," I hissed and she rolled out from under the car, a headlamp on her forehead.

"What?" she whispered, holding up a wrench and some other contraption like it should be obvious what she was doing.

"What are we doing here?"

"I'm taking back what's mine." She shrugged, then slid back under the car. I got on my hands and knees, peering under the car towards her.

"You're taking some part?"

"Something like that. This is his ... I dunno, regular car, I guess. But I still did a shit ton of free work on it. So I'm taking it back." She worked as she spoke, setting up a tray and draining out the oil. While that went on, she moved towards the front of the car and undid a headlight.

I watched quietly as she undid all her work on this car, occasionally handing her tools or taking a part from her to set it aside. Something about this silence was different. I got the feeling she was working through something that I shouldn't interrupt. Even though we were invading on private property and I was anxious to get out of here.

"I can't remember the last time he said thank you for any of the work I did on the cars. Back when he did say it, I'd always reply, 'Don't mention it, I love working on cars.' I'd meant it but when I noticed he stopped saying thank you, I felt ... I dunno, unloved, I guess. It was like I did this time-consuming thing because it made his life easier or better and because I loved him. And he didn't even acknowledge it."

I didn't reply. Zoey was under the car again, but I wasn't sure she was doing anything in particular. Just clanging around. Like she wanted to be heard.

"This is a small town, lots of high school sweethearts stay together, get married, have kids. I expected the same of us. But after he graduated college and got his first 'real' job and there was no ring, I ... I don't know. That wasn't a thing you asked. It's not *ladylike* to nag about marriage. And what if asking made him not want to marry me? Nobody else had ever liked me, I couldn't lose him. So I stayed quiet. Fat lot of good that did me."

Zoey kicked at her toolbox, sending everything clanging out. The back door shot open to reveal a very tall, very angry, very not Johnny man.

"Whoever the fuck is out there, I've called the sheriff!" he shouted.

"Fuck off, Grant!" Zoey shouted back, not moving out from under the car. "Call Joey back and tell him not to bother. He'd be on my side anyways."

"Zoey? Fucking Christ. Have you not caused enough trouble already?"

"Ask the bastard your housing."

"You and I know damn well he couldn't live with his parents. What was I supposed to do? Let my cousin sleep on the streets?"

"Sounds like the consequences of his actions."

"God damn it," the man muttered before turning back into the house and shouting, "Johnny, this is your mess to deal with."

Johnny showed up at the back door just as blue light shone from the front lawn.

"What the fuck, Zoey? You've not fucked up my life enough already? Now you're — what? Cutting my breaks or some shit? Trying to sabotage my car for the race?"

Zoey'd pulled out from under the car and sat up, arms crossed, glaring at Johnny.

"You cheated on me. You don't get to decide when I've ruined your life enough," she spat. Zoey stood, kicking at the wheeled tray she'd been using. "And I know you're not using this car for the race, asshole. You don't know much, but you at least know how to pick a car."

"Then what the fuck are you doing?" Johnny started down the steps, jaw set in a way that made me step in front of Zoey.

"All right, y'all, let's cool it down," a new man, dressed in a brown sheriff's uniform said as he stepped into the backyard. "How 'bout y'all tell me what's going on and then we just talk it out?"

While the accent was thick and the uniform ... not particularly ironed straight, I did appreciate how he stepped in front of Johnny, blocking the man's view of Zoey.

"She's fucking with my car, man. Ask her."

"Ms. Riggs?" the man said, turning to face Zoey, who rolled her eyes. I suppose respect for law enforcement was … low in Snowfall. Or maybe it was just these two. It was hard to tell. I'll have to ask Rosie, she seemed to have the most sense of the group.

"Mr. Clark here hasn't paid for any of the auto maintenance on this vehicle since it was purchased. Since it seems he's unable or unwilling to pay the invoice, I'm remedying the matter by undoing any the work."

The Sheriff nodded as Zoey spoke, but Johnny stepped around him. "Invoice? I never got an invoice."

"Oh, it must have gotten mailed to your old address. Here's a copy," Zoey said, stepping around me to hand Johnny a stack of folded papers. And when she returned to my side, she had the most bitter smile I'd ever seen. I'd have been scared of her if I was Johnny.

"Old address? You know I live here, you fucking TP'd the house after *stealing* my car," Johnny said as he shifted through the papers.

"Now, Johnny, I remember you calling in about that car. But her name's on the title. She has just as much a legal right to it as you do," the Sheriff droned, Johnny ignored him.

"I can't believe you lied about calling the cops. What a bitch move," Zoey grumbled while Johnny read the invoice, eyes widening.

"What the fuck are with these prices? I'm not paying this shit." Johnny tossed the papers aside and the Sheriff picked them back up.

"No, sir. These are standard prices. And considering the oldest charge listed is a year old and there's no interest charge, this is a fair deal."

"I figured the free labor stopped the second you started cheating on me. I just guessed at a date, but I have a feeling it's been longer than a year. Do you wanna confirm that? Or how many women there've been? Or would you rather I take you to court for the unpaid bills? Ashley specialized in financial law, so I'm sure she could make this a lot more difficult than dealing with the undone work. Or you can pay the bill and I'll fix everything back up, no additional charge. That'd be cheaper than going to court too."

"Who's Ashley?" Johnny said, the blankest look on his dumb ass face. He didn't answer any of the questions Zoey threw at him, he didn't show a sign of remorse, and he couldn't even remember one of her friend's names.

All right, sir, let's remember to take a breath."

I hadn't realized I'd started walking toward Johnny until the Sheriff put a gentle hand on my chest.

"Now, Johnny," the Sheriff started, turning to the man in question. "Everybody's heard the rumors, seen them stickers. We know what you did. And you're not gonna find many folks on your side on this matter. Sometimes folks do stupid shit and other folks wanna see 'em face the consequences. That's just the way of things. I'm also not trained for this sorta counseling, so you're barking up the wrong tree. If you wanna talk this out, you do it with a third-party mediator. Ideally not in the middle of the night. But I guess if you can find a counselor willing to do it, I'm not one to judge."

The Sheriff continued looking at Johnny for a minute longer before turning to Zoey.

"Now, Zoey. It's quite late for you to be causin' a ruckus in somebody's private yard. I suggest you let Mr. Clark sleep on the matter and you call it a night. Sound fair?"

Zoey dropped her arms and sighed. Without a word, she turned back to the car and started gathering up her tools.

"Fat lot of good you cops do," Johnny muttered before stomping back to his house. The Sheriff and I watched him go before it was my turn to be addressed.

"You Ms. Riggs' new man?" he asked and I immediately nodded. I was her man. In some type of way, I was hers. It didn't really matter how. "Right, well I know you're probably tryin' to help her heal and whatnot, but do me a favor and try and temper her down some. That dumba— I mean, Mr. Clark has a tendency to call us over things we can't control, like what happened with The Paper."

"What happened with The Paper?" I asked, face as blank as I could make it. The Sheriff raised his brow at me then shook his head.

"Yeah, sure. Y'all get home safe. Try to save your trouble for after the Valentine's Fest, at least. We're gonna have too many drunk single folks to deal with to handle this sorta mess," he grumbled as he walked off to the front yard. From behind me, Zoey nudged me in the back.

"Let's go. I got everything undone and it's not like he was ever gonna answer me anyways." She trudged back to the car and I followed. But as she was tossing her tool bags into the back, I slid into the driver's seat. I was readjusting the seat and mirrors when she came up and opened the door. "Uh, what're you doing?"

"Driving you home." Zoey made a disgruntled face, but before she could argue with me anymore, I added, "It's mine turn to drive. Your turn to rest. You need it."

Zoey opened her mouth, closed it, opened it again, then just shook her head and rounded the car to sit on the passenger side.

It was a short, quiet ride. And as much as I wanted to verbally check in on her, I knew it wasn't time. Those questions she'd asked had probably taken her months to get out. And for all the bravery she'd shown in asking them, she got nothing for it. So when I finally parked in Zoey's drive, I decided this was the time for a distraction instead of a talk. "Do you want to go to that Valentine's Day thing with me?"

18

'CONSTRUCTIVE CONCERN'

ZOEY

Olivia: Diner. Now.

Olivia: And no Stephen

Me: 1) why? 2) it's not like I bring Stephen with me everywhere. He's only been here, like, a week

Olivia: Shut up and get your ass over here

Me: But what'll I do with Stephen?

Olivia: Zoey, I swear to god, if you're not in this diner in ten minutes, I'm coming to your house and taking every goddamn car key you have and tossing them from the lookout

Me: You wouldn't dare

Olivia: Try me

I stepped into the diner six minutes later. Not because I thought Olivia would follow through on her threat but ... just in case.

All of my friends were crowded into the back corner booth, next to the jukebox. It had been our spot since middle school. For study sessions and milkshakes, gossip rants and pancakes, and ... interventions and spiked milkshakes.

And my orange creamsicle milkshake was right there waiting for me.

God. Damn. It.

I should've known it was coming. There was only so much town chaos I could cause without getting a 'friendly' talking to. Especially since I'd skipped out on the last town hall. I'd contemplated asking Shea to livestream it, but then I'd have to explain why and I much preferred not having to acknowledge Johnny's suffering. It wasn't worth acknowledging yet.

I don't know when it would feel worth it.

"All right, let's get this over with," I grumbled as I took my seat in the booth next to Roxie.

"You stole a car, Zoey! Without telling us! You don't have the right to cop an attitude," Olivia said, leaning into the table to stare me down. I should appreciate the concern, the willingness to call me out on my shit in an attempt to keep me from burning myself down. But I couldn't *feel* it. There was just a hole where that emotion should be.

"I don't think criticizing how she's grieving is gonna help any," Roxie said with a click of her tongue.

"I wouldn't call plastering stickers saying 'Johnny cheats for blowjobs' grieving. But it was fucking hilarious," Shea said, taking a loud slurp from her milkshake and holding out a hand for me to high-five.

I couldn't leave her hanging. Or fight the grin I got from remembering the way Stephen carefully picked out places to put them while I slapped them wherever I could reach.

"Stephen made those for me."

"Aw," Rosie crooned, getting an elbow from Olivia. "Oh, hush, it is kinda sweet. Don't you think?"

"It's kinda a crime," Olivia argued.

"Eh, worst she'd get is community service," Ashley piped up, making a face like she was already planning what argument she would make to a judge.

"And the car thing?" Olivia argued.

"Her name is on the title." Ashley shrugged. "She has full legal rights to the vehicle and a key. You read the report, the police aren't going to do anything about it."

"Report?" I repeated.

"Oh yeah, you missed *a lot* at the town hall. Ms. Taylor sorta read a list of your 'crimes' and a rather ... handsy argument broke out," Shea explained, still slurping at her drink. It probably had more than ice cream in it. "Is the squirrel thing true?"

I nodded and Shea melted in a fit of laughter, leaning into Olivia, who shoved her off. Rosie pushed both their drinks across the table and away from flailing hands.

"This is serious," Olivia whined, though the last word went high as she giggled and smacked Shea to stop tickling her.

"We're just worried that all these ... revenge plots aren't going to help you in the long run," Rosie said, pushing at Shea from over Olivia.

"The real problem is that Johnny's being a bitch and reporting you. He should just take his punishment like a fucking man," Ashley grumbled.

"Like Mason does for you?" Shea asked, wiggling her brows.

"He's less of a bitch than Johnny, I'll admit that much."

The whole tabled uh-huh'd her and she rolled her eyes.

"Whatever. We're talking about Zoey," she grumbled, taking a sip of her strawberry shake.

"There's nothing to talk about. I'm fine. Joey said I was within my legal rights last night, so no problems there."

There was a beat where I thought nobody noticed. I mean, I very well could have talked to Joey last night over the phone. Except ...

"When'd you talk to Sheriff Joey? After our talk? That was, like, well after midnight," Roxie asked, one perfect brow raised.

"... it was after."

"What'd you call Rox about?" Olivia asked, her voice dropping.

"She had some sex questions. Why would Joey call you after midnight? ... unless Johnny had a new complaint."

"Are you having sex with Stephen without telling me?" Olivia shouted.

"No," I said, the same time Roxie said, "Yeah."

"Roxie," I shouted, nudging her with my shoulder.

"What? You did."

"No, we did ... not sex."

"Oh, I figured you were gonna fuck Stephen after that call. But I'd still call what you did sex. It's still sexual intimacy even if there was no penetration."

"Zoey!" Olivia cried.

"What?"

"What did you do with this stranger that you can't tell your best friend about?"

"Oh my god, it's not that big of a deal, we just sorta ... took turns getting off in front of each other."

"What?" the whole table, except Roxie, screeched.

"That seems hella intimate for a dude you just met," Shea said, whistling before retrieving her milkshake.

"No. Roxie said it was normal."

"I said it was a common thing partners do. I *didn't* say it wasn't intimate. It's pretty damn intimate. I don't think I've ever done it."

"What?"

"Are you actually *with* Stephen? Where did he say he lived again? What're you gonna do when his car gets fixed? Isn't this too soon after Johnny?" Olivia asked, spiraling in a way only she was capable of.

"I'm not *with* him, we're just sorta ... I dunno. It doesn't matter. Can we talk about literally anything else?"

There was a long, tense silence at the table, eyes shifting between one another, but mostly focused on me and Olivia.

"Why didn't you include us in any of it?" she asked quietly.

Shame.

It was an easy answer. One I'm sure Olivia was smart enough to figure out on her own.

Because what the fuck *was* I doing? Pulling all these stupid pranks, putting myself at legal risk, dragging a decent man into my mess. And what did I even have to show for all that trouble? Johnny might be pissed, he might have to sink more money into his car, but that was it. He didn't have to face the same consequences I did. He didn't have to do the work to move on like I did. He didn't even have to answer the questions like I have.

It was embarrassing that I was in this situation to begin with. Even more embarrassing how I was handling it.

And I hated the way it all burned.

So I did the simplest thing I could do. I left.

A series of shouts followed me, but the only thing I could pick out before the bells over the door drowned everything out was Rosie saying, "Let's give her a bit more space."

19

PENSIVE ANNOUNCEMENTS NECESSITATE COMFORT, ASSURANCES, KISSES, AND, EVENTUALLY, SEX

STEPHEN

I spent an embarrassing amount of time waiting for Zoey to come home after her girls' night. I think it took nearly a whole season of Supernatural for me to give up and go to bed.

I wasn't worried about her. She was out with friends, friends she had been close with since elementary school. She probably got caught up talking with them and forgot to let me know she'd be staying at one of their houses.

It was just that the house was lonely without her.

So when I got up the next morning, the first thing I did was reach for my phone hoping she had texted me.

She hadn't. But there was one message from Roxie, outside of the group chat which had too many unread messages to touch, that caught my eye.

> **Roxie:** Our girl's having a hard time, but she trusts you with something she isn't trusting us with. Do me a favor and watch out for her, okay?

I read the text a few times over, not understanding what she meant. Why would she text me if Zoey was with her or one of the others in the friend group?

Then I walked into the kitchen and looked out the window.

Zoey was in the garage in the backyard, hair tied up in a high ponytail, grease covering her face, and rolling a tire out the garage door to crash in the yard. Tire 'disposed' of, she clapped her hands and went back into the garage, out of sight. I tried to figure out what she was doing based on the small glimpses I could catch of her through the window but whatever she was up to was far beyond my knowledge of car maintenance. I could tell she was focused though. Completely in her own world as she worked.

Logic said to let her be. I'd never been keen on how Darren interrupted me in the middle of work. Probably one of the bigger arguments we'd had was over how he'd interrupted me while I was focused on my senior thesis at 4:00 am because he thought I hadn't eaten that day/the day before.

I hadn't. Which was probably why the argument had gotten as bad as it did.

And Roxie did tell me to take care of Zoey. Maybe now was the time to talk about those questions she didn't get answers to.

After asking Rosie for her pancake recipe, and receiving strict instructions not to share it with anyone, I spent the next hour making Zoey the tallest stack of pancakes I could manage, which turned out to be 30. Anymore and I think they'd end up on the floor the second I stepped out of the kitchen.

"Zoey?" I called as I stepped into the garage, the plate of pancakes held with *both* hands.

Zoey was on a stool leaning over to work on the engine of a car that ... looked fast. It was one of the old cars where the door hinged at the top. Maybe the *Back to the Future* car. Except with bright purple and white stripes along the sides. It certainly looked cool.

"Hey, Stephen. I'll be done in an hour or two," Zoey said without turning around. She was in the shirt she wore last night, a working jumpsuit over her clothes with the sleeves tied at her waist. There were several black splotches across the jumpsuit, but one particular set of fingerprints along her waist made me burn. It was all too easy to imagine them as Johnny's hands on her waist. Her ass.

I shook my head, trying to leave those thoughts behind as I stepped closer to Zoey to touch her elbow. Her eyes met mine, bright and teary, nose an irritated red.

"You've been crying." An obvious statement but ... it was different from before. It wasn't anger or frustration. She hadn't been running around throwing shit, she'd been quiet in her work. And quiet Zoey and tears meant something was wrong.

"You bought me pancakes," she stated, voice soft and dull.

"No, I made them for you. Rosie's recipe."

"Rosie gave you her pancake recipe?" Zoey asked, voice cracking. She reached a hand out, but I pulled the plate away giving her grease-covered hands a dubious look. Her lips pulled just a smidge before she rolled her eyes and went to the sink in the back corner of the garage. She returned, with clean hands, and immediately scarfed down a pancake. While on her second one, she closed the hood of her car and took a seat, patting the metal beside her. I took my seat, setting the plate of pancakes carefully between us.

"This," Zoey tapped the hood of the car, "is the last car my dad and I bought at an auction before he started getting sick. My dad taught Johnny everything the prick knows about driving. Dad liked racing cars just as much as he liked rebuilding them. I'm kinda indifferent about the whole racing thing, so they bonded over that. If Dad were alive he'd probably run over Johnny. Since he can't, I figured the next best thing is to beat him in this car. Dad had a list of things he wanted to do with it. Wish I still had it around. He always thought of the most random shit to do."

I ate a pancake in silence, waiting for her to continue, knowing she would if I gave her the space to.

The pancakes turned out really good though.

"I keep waiting for that feeling of retribution or whatever to come, for all these stupid revenge schemes to work. But they never do. I see Johnny's reactions and they don't bring me any sort of joy because I know his misery is temporary. He'll get over it and I'll be stuck in this tornado of misery, empty on the inside. I hate it. I didn't do anything wrong, I shouldn't be the miserable one. I miss being happy. I miss not worrying about people pitying me. I miss being myself. I don't know how to get myself back. I'm not even sure if I know who I am without him."

I dropped the half-eaten pancake to take Zoey by the shoulder and turned her to face me.

"Zoey Riggs, you are so much more than who you were with him. I don't even know that person. But the Zoey I know is too generous for her own good, willing to say shit others aren't because they don't wanna ruffle feathers, and will fight anyone who has wronged someone she loves. You are kind and compassionate. And you tell the stupidest jokes that I think only you can tell and still be charming. And you're so damn smart and passionate. You've got the kind of passion that's contagious. While you were shopping for parts, I spent the whole time looking up shit to understand what you were talking about.

"I know he took a piece of you, stole it, but it wasn't all of you. Not even close."

Zoey took my words in, big watery eyes softening as she listened. And when I finished, her hands cupped my cheeks, eyes falling to my lips.

"You really are smooth, aren'tcha?" she whispered, one corner of her mouth tipping up.

"You're the only one that thinks so."

"Hmm. I don't know about that. I used to think nobody else would ever see me as a woman. You know, the whole tomboy, into cars thing didn't attract the guys like I thought it would in high school. But you see me." It wasn't a question. Zoey knew and was confident in the fact that I found her attractive. As she should be.

"Am I allowed to like you while I'm still not —"

I put a finger over her lips to keep her from saying his name. Then pulled back before she had a chance to bite me this time. Zoey smiled, knowing exactly what I was thinking.

"Yes. Whatever makes you happy."

Zoey's hands dropped from my face to my shoulders and she pulled herself on top of me, knocking the pancakes between us to the floor.

How did I know those were going to fall?

It was hard to mourn the loss of pancakes when Zoey settled herself on top of me, her arms wrapped around my neck.

"If I kiss you, are you gonna stop me this time?" she asked, spreading her legs so she was pressed against me, as close as she could get.

Ignoring the rush of blood, I leaned back to get a good look at Zoey. This only made her press against my cock in a deliciously different way.

"Are you sure you want this right now?" I somehow managed, even as I leaned back further, fully laying on the hood, Zoey straddled on top of me.

"Yes. I want to do something that'll make me happy, something that doesn't involve him. That something is you." My hands went to her waist as she rested her hands on either side of me, eyes eating me up. She pushed back on her knees, then took each of my wrists in a hand to pin them over me. "Will you let me?"

I'm never leaving Snowfall, am I?

"Yes, pretty girl. Use me for whatever you need."

Zoey's lips crashed to mine with more roughness and fervor than after trivia. And I met her with just as much need, if not more because nothing had been dulling my desire beyond respect for her space. But now there was nothing holding me back. ... except her hands holding my wrists over my head. I wouldn't fight her on that though. I liked her taking what she needed from me, however that was. Fuck, she could tie me down if she really wanted to and I'd happily hold my hands out for her.

But as her kisses heated from quick and needy to slow exploration, her hands dropped away to slide up my shirt. I took advantage of my free hands, grabbing her by the waist and sitting up so I could pull her tight against me. She rocked into me, whimpering into my mouth as she grinded into my erection. I'm not sure if I've ever heard a hotter sound in my life. But with her rubbing on me like that, I needed to move things to a bed, quickly.

Grabbing her by the ass, I slid us off the car, ready to carry her back inside and to her bed. No, the guest bed. Fuck that bed and the time she spent in it with Johnny.

"Stephen," Zoey whined, her lips barely leaving mine as she tugged at the collar of my shirt. "Where're we going?"

"To a bed, pretty girl." Zoey immediately shook her head and my heart dropped. I'd resisted taking care of myself after all our moments so far, minus when she asked to watch. But that wouldn't be the case this time. I was too on. Too full of her. I needed some release, even if I couldn't have it with her. "That's all right. No bed. Whatever you need, pretty girl. Just tell me what you want to do, how far you want to take this."

"No," she groaned, putting a hand out to grab the door frame of the garage. "I wanna have sex here." With her legs wrapped around my waist, she grinded into me. "Now."

"In the garage?"

"Yes."

"But the ..." I nodded to the open door.

"No one can see us from the front of the house. Please. I need you. *Now*."

I'm a good listener. And an especially eager listener when it came to pleasing Zoey.

I turned us back around and set her ass on the hood of the car. With her legs, Zoey pulled me closer, hands digging into my shirt to tug my lips back to hers.

"Where're the condoms?" I asked. I was barely able to keep my mouth off her. She was so fucking sweet, I needed to memorize this taste.

"I don't want one. Just fuck me, Stephen. Stop with the questions and fuck me." She pulled at my shirt, dragging it over my head.

"But —"

"No. This is what I want. And when I'm with you, I get what I want, right?" She looked up at me, hands on the button of my jeans. Her eyes were so dark with need, that they pulled me in, drowned me.

"Okay, but what about —"

"I'm on the pill. And if you get me pregnant from a .01 percent chance ... well you better make it worth it. I wanna come at least three times. And if I don't and I do get pregnant, I want extra child support or whatever. So if you can agree to those odds, just .. whip it out."

I buried my face in her neck, trying to stifle my laughter.

I definitely wasn't leaving Snowfall.

"I'll take those odds, pretty girl. Let's get these off first." I tugged at the arms of her overalls, undoing the knot at her waist. "I don't like seeing another man's hand prints on you."

Zoey tilted to the side, looking down at the stain in question. She smacked her hands down on the hood and lifted her hips.

"Then take them off and make your own."

I tore the clothes down her legs and tossed them somewhere, hopefully near the garbage. "Be careful what you wish for, pretty girl. I've been told

I'm a menace when I'm focused on something. And I have a feeling it'll be especially bad with you."

Without giving her a chance to snark back, I took her lips. I took her lips and kissed her with all the need I'd felt over the last few days. The need hadn't been words, just desire. But now I knew what it was. It was the need to make her feel better, make her forget, make her mine.

That's how I kissed her. Like she was already completely mine.

And I planned to fuck her like that too. Like she'd been mine all along and this amazing blaze inside me was what it was like every time we were together. Because I truly believed it would always feel like this. No matter if this ended up being a one-off and I'd have to wait months or years to have her again. She'd be mine eventually, in the same way I was already hers.

Dragging my teeth over her lips, I skimmed down to her neck, sucking at the skin under her ear, a piece of me dying inside at the sound she made in response. My hands raked over her body, finding the softness of her stomach and sliding my hand into her underwear, going down through coarse curls until I found the wet warmth between her legs. Taking my time, I explored her with light touches, memorizing her shape, how she shivered as I massaged her lips, the way she cried when I finally pressed against her clit. I massaged slow circles into her as I continued my perusal of her neck, searching for the spot that'd get the best reaction. When I found it, I sunk my teeth into her, marking her and the spot I'd always come back to whenever we were together.

"Stephen," she whined, the last half of my name coming out with a shiver as I began to kiss the bite mark. Zoey's hands dug into my hair, pulling me closer. "Stop toying with me."

"As you wish, pretty girl," I whispered into her ear as I slid my finger lower and into her. She was so damn hot and wet and perfect.

"Tell me this is all for me, Zoey," I pleaded, stroking her while my palm grinded against her clit. Now that I could feel her, actually feel her, I needed to *feel* her come around my fingers as soon as possible.

"I guess," she answered between breathy moans.

"You guess?" I chuckled, quickening the pace of my fingers.

"Well, it's also pretty hot doing this on the car that I'm gonna race, like we're christening it. So that's a part of it." Her words came out ragged as I added another finger. Her hips rocked into me and I matched her pace. She was so damn close, pulsing erratically around my fingers, dragging her nails through my hair.

"Christen this ride then, Zoey. Show me how my pretty girl comes on my fingers."

"Fuck, Stephen," she gasped, gripping my clothes frantically as she rode my fingers. I buried my free hand in her hair and pulled just enough so that I could meet her eyes. Meet her eyes and watch them roll back as she came.

"So fucking pretty," I murmured to myself, watching her body spasm. "So fucking perfect."

When she came down, breaths evening, her eyes returned to mine, the brightest shade of blue I'd ever seen. Sparkling, she was sparkling with the release and it was a sight I was going to need to see again and again, for the rest of my life.

And I was especially eager to see it from between her legs.

"Woah, wait, what're you doing?" Zoey asked, the last word going high as I sank to my knees and yanked her panties down.

"I'm going to make you come again." I pulled at her knees and she shut them.

"No, I — you don't have to do it like that, your cock is more than enough to get the job done, trust me. Plus I haven't shaved in a while, so we can just move on to the big shebang." Her hand moved to cover herself, but I grabbed it before she could hide my meal.

"I'm not particularly keen on waiting any longer to get a taste of you."

"You tasted me on the toy, so —"

"That isn't enough and you know it," I interrupted, the words coming out grittier than I intended. But if she thought that measly taste was enough to satisfy my need for her, she was insane. "So unless you have a real reason why I shouldn't eat you out, I'm going to insist." I tossed her hand towards her side and pulled her knees apart. This time she didn't immediately close them, but she did bite at her lip.

"Well, I ... doesn't the hair get in the way?"

"No." I didn't bother explaining further. I'd rather prove my point another way. But what she'd said about my cock being enough reminded me of something. And with the smell of her sweet, drenched pussy making me cocky, I couldn't help but tease her.

"Plus you said I was bigger than you're used to. So I have an obligation to make sure you're properly prepared for me, Zoey. I wouldn't want to hurt you." I waited until she was rolling her eyes to drag my tongue up her pussy.

Just the smell of her had my mouth watering, but the taste ... *fuck*. I pulled at her waist, angling her up so I could get more of her. It was hard to tell if it was because of that orange-honey soap or if it was just her, but Zoey was so damn sweet. I could eat her out every day and I'm not sure it'd be enough.

"Ambrosia, pretty girl. You taste like ambrosia," I murmured into her, sliding two fingers into her pussy as I teased her clit with my tongue. Slow circles turned to rough passes turned to quick flicks. The need to make her come quickening my pace.

"I ... I don't — fuck, what does that mean?" she said between gasps. Her fingers sank into my hair, pulling at the strands like it was all she could do to hold on.

"The drink of the gods, Zoey. You're fucking divine."

Zoey's whole body tensed and, with great difficulty, I pulled away to meet her gaze. There was something soft in her eyes, something I couldn't quite name.

"You really mean that?" she asked, voice still hoarse from her first orgasm.

Logically, I knew that her doubt didn't come from me. She had a shit partner her whole adult life and he'd done far too much damage. There was no way for me to undo it all, not with the little time we'd had so far. But one day. One day there wouldn't be a single doubt in that pretty, wild mind of hers that I enjoyed giving her pleasure. All types of pleasure.

But for now, I'd keep it simple.

"Yes. I do." I kept my eyes on hers as I resumed fingering her, keeping my pace slow until my lips returned to her clit. Then I sucked hard.

Zoey screamed my name with a fervor that I relished. So I kept her screaming. I kept stroking and sucking until her warmth dripped down my fingers. It was only then that I gave her swollen clit a rest so that I could lap up her come. She shivered as I cleaned her up, alternating between pulling me closer and tugging me away, like everything was on the brink of being too much for her.

When I was satisfied, I trailed my lips up her body, pressing soft kisses against the softest bits of skin. Her thighs, the dip of her waist where my hands settled so nicely, her stomach, pulling up her shirt to kiss the bottom curve of her breasts.

Every soft part of hers was mine to care for right now. Not just her body but all the softness she'd shown me since I crashed into this town. The tears, the feelings, the soft admissions she told me but not her friends. I would take care of all of it.

"Stephen, that was ... I didn't ..." Zoey murmured as my face came level with hers. I kissed each cheek, waiting to see if she'd be able to gather her senses enough to form a sentence. I selfishly hoped she wouldn't be able to.

"I don't think I've ever come that hard."

Well, that was certainly a close second to rendering her speechless.

"Don't worry, Zoey, we'll fix that too. Think you're ready for me now?"

Instead of answering me, Zoey pushed up, leaning into me to yank my pants down. Laughing, I joined her to strip me of my remaining clothes before tearing off her shirt. Her breasts, small and soft and beautiful, rose with her heavy breaths. I needed to taste them too.

"Stephen," Zoey grumbled as I began to lick her nipple. She slid her fingers up my neck and gripped my hair to pull me up. "Stop getting distracted and fuck me."

I nipped at her hardened nipple before letting her pull me away.

"I wouldn't say I was distracted. You said you liked your nipples played. I told you I was attentive."

"Oh my god, just give me your cock. For fucks sake. Or are you gonna make me beg for it or some shit because if that's the case, you can —"

Zoey was so caught up with her grumbles, she didn't notice I'd resituated my hands so one was on her waist while the other lined up my cock. Then I yanked her ass down across the hood of the car and onto my cock.

"Fuck," we hissed in unison, our foreheads resting against each other and Zoey's arms wrapping behind my neck. She hugged me closer, shifting her waist so I could slide in deeper.

She's fucking heaven.

And before I had a moment to breathe her in, to get used to the tightness of her pussy, the warmth of her, Zoey started rocking her hips. Hand sinking into the hair at the nape of her neck, I pulled her away to meet her eyes.

"Not so fast, pretty girl. I need to make you come at least one more time. Not that I'm opposed to continuing pleasing you after I've come, but I wanna enjoy being inside you a little longer." Zoey's pussy fluttered around me and I had to squeeze my eyes shut to keep from coming.

Once I'd regained my composure, I let go of her hair to reposition her. One leg on each of my shoulders, ass on the edge of the hood, pussy full of my cock. I bent my pretty girl in half and fucked her.

Despite all my thoughts about being tender and soft with her, I simply couldn't now that my cock was involved. And Zoey only spurred me on, little whimpers and pleas for more or harder or just unintelligible mumbles that I instinctively knew the meaning of. I fulfilled her every request, met every demand, and was rewarded with the erratic squeezing of her release.

I grinded into her, moving one hand to gently rub her clit. Then just as her breathing started to even out again, I increased the pressure on her clit and rammed into her. Zoey cursed, then screamed my name, nails running down my back.

I hope they leave a mark. Her hickey's already starting to bloom, it's only fair she marks me too.

"Stephen, please," she murmured into my ear between pants.

"Please what?" My voice came out ragged, sweat dripping into my eyes. There was no way I could hold on much longer. But I wanted to feel her come around my cock one more time. Just one more time.

"Come with me this time," she whispered. And fuck if I could deny her.

"As you wish, pretty girl."

20

PAPER HEARTS

ZOEY

When I woke up the next day, cuddling Stephen's back like he was a giant teddy bear that had the magic ability to scare away any nightmare, I felt settled for the first time in months. It could have been the several orgasms I had yesterday or the fact that I hadn't woken up in the middle of the night for once. But I knew it was Stephen.

And that knowledge freaked me the fuck out.

And it made my heart go all warm and gooey.

So I snuck out of bed, ignoring Stephen's cute little grumble as he patted my side of the bed to find it empty, and texted my best friend.

> **Me:** I like Stephen, what do I do about it?

Then I remembered how I'd stormed out the other night and braced myself for a passive-aggressive response.

> **Olivia:** Like as in you have a crush on him or like as in you're gonna start dating?

I let out a long sigh of relief. She was going to let me have this moment without hashing out what happened. The world was full of blessings today.

Me: What's the difference?

Olivia: Him liking you back

Olivia: Though I guess that's a stupid question, he clearly has a thing for you

Me: Obviously, I'm a catch

Olivia: Of course you are. But does that mean you're dating him?

Me: I guess?

Olivia: YOU GUESS?!?!?! WTF does that mean?

Me: Well he said he was willing to do long distance before

Me: But we didn't actually confirm it

Me: I'm gonna go with yes

Me: Is that right?

Olivia: I'm not the one who can answer that. But I'm happy for you. Stephen seems nice. Even if he doesn't talk much in the group chat

Me: What group chat?

Olivia: …

Olivia: We just wanted a chat so we could all keep an eye on him

Olivia: And so that he could let us know if you got into any … legal trouble

Me: I can't believe y'all have a group chat without me

Me: With my maybe boyfriend

Olivia: In my defense, you've been doing a lot of questionable things lately and he's the only one you're letting keep an eye on you

Olivia: Besides if he is your boyfriend, especially long distance, we'll need a way to harass him

Me: Why are you already anticipating needing to harass my maybe long distance boyfriend?

Olivia: I dunno. If he doesn't call or visit enough or if you had a really bad day but don't tell him because he has a stressful meeting coming up or something

Me: Stop trying to spread your anxiety around

Olivia: Yeah, I'll be sure to do that. Just after I solve world hunger

Oh shit. It was Valentine's Day.

I rolled my eyes before typing a quick 'we'll see' and tossing my phone on the couch. She was right, I may bitch about the Valentine's Fest being corny as fuck, but it was cute and over-the-top gushy and that stupid kind of cheesy that felt right when you were in love.

To be honest, I only complained about it because that's what everybody expected of the tomboy. Johnny certainly liked to complain about it. I think he only went because his mother would have his ass if he didn't. And I didn't wanna be another person forcing him into it.

But ...

"There's my pretty girl," Stephen said as he walked into the living room, his voice rough from sleep.

Pretty girl.

It wasn't a common term of endearment, it was simple, and I'm not sure it suited me at all. But Stephen did. *That* made the little nickname special.

"You sleep well?" he asked, sinking into the couch beside me, and immediately resting his head on my shoulder. As if it was an old habit, he squeezed my knee, then reached for the remote and turned on our next episode of Supernatural. He'd confessed he'd watched a whole season without me and I gave him a lot of shit for it. I'd seen it before, but it was fun teasing him.

"I did. You?" Stephen smiled, brightly, like he remembered me talking about my insomnia and took note that it didn't happen when I slept next to him. Cocky bastard.

"Yeah, I slept well too." He settled back onto the couch, head returning to my shoulder. And just like that, we watched the monster of the week attack some unsuspecting person.

"Hey, Stephen?"

"Uh-huh?"

"You're my boyfriend now, right?" I didn't look away from the screen, but I could feel him look at me, could imagine his brow raised for a second before a smile spread. Picturing that smile made me turn. And it warmed my heart to see him just as I expected, smiling crookedly up at me.

"Yeah, I'm your boyfriend." He took my hand, pressing a kiss to my knuckles. "And you're my girlfriend now, right?"

I sighed dramatically, making him laugh. But then I twisted our entwined hands and kissed his knuckles.

"Yeah, I'm your girlfriend." I set our hands back in my lap then added, "So don't be a dick to me or your car's never getting fixed."

Stephen threw his head back and laughed. The sound was relaxing, a surprise given how he snorted, but comforting nonetheless. So I said exactly what I wanted.

"I wanna go to the Valentine's Fest tonight."

Another lazy smile. "I thought that was already the plan."

"It was? Since when? We literally just decided to be a couple."

"I asked if you wanted to go after you trespassed and deconstructed a car. You said yes."

"Hmm. Yeah, I definitely wasn't paying attention." Stephen chuckled, a light laugh that I read as 'that's my silly girlfriend'. So I continued, "But you can't just ask someone you're not dating to the Valentine's Fest! That's like illegal, maybe."

"Illegal?" he repeated.

"Okay, maybe not illegal-illegal like some of the shit I've done. But you'd get a shit ton of dirty looks if you go with somebody you aren't dating." I rolled my eyes and nudged my elbow into Stephen's ribs. "It's a big deal. A shit ton of tourists come in, all the stores have special little booths. Not sure what Dennis is gonna do, nothing really romantic about bikes. But anyway, they decorate the whole downtown with flowers and streamers and shit. There are hot chocolate booths and candy apples and cotton candy in the shape of hearts. And you're supposed to fill out these lil' paper hearts. The couple's name goes on the front then it gets folded in half and each person writes something for their partner to read next year. They get hung up all over the walls and hang from the gazebo. They've collected like a million over the years, so it's like a cloud of pink and red covers the town. It's just … really pretty. But kinda girly and mushy. So I get if you're not interested anymore knowing all that."

I hated that I cushioned the whole thing, that I gave him an out, that the brace for disappointment was instinctual. Why hadn't I noticed all the times I did that for Johnny? All the times I let what he would prefer dictate what I wanted? Why did I do that for a man who never took me into consideration? Was I really so fucking stupid that —

"That sounds fun. Let's go make a heart," Stephen said, squeezing my knee. I looked at him from the corner of my eyes, trying to tell if he knew I'd gone into a mental rage tornado or not. Probably. He was a perceptive little bastard.

I guess I like that about him.

"Don't look," I shouted, slapping Stephen's arm as his hand started to tilt the folded heart to peek at what I wrote.

"But I'm curious," was his simple response.

"It's bad luck if you look before next year."

Stephen grumbled but set the folded heart, my side down, on the table so he could write. As he wrote I shifted my feet closer, leaning in so I could see a straight-edged L. Stephen cleared his throat, raising an eyebrow at me. I just shrugged and turned away to look at the rest of the downtown strip while Stephen finished writing.

I'd been slightly worried that after talking up the festival, it would have somehow been canceled or less extravagant than it usually was. But if there was one thing Ms. Taylor took pride in, it was her festivals. And this Valentine's Fest was no exception. Though I did suspect she pulled out all the stops because her grandkid just got back from her honeymoon.

There was a large flower wall set up near the gazebo, pink and red and purple roses all tended to by the local florist, Abigail. Between couples taking pictures, she fluffed and sprayed and adjusted hearts pinned to the wall in a nervous manner. She was a few years younger than me, so I didn't know her that well, but I got the feeling she was bullied into this by Ms. Taylor. Every time she thought no one was looking, Abigail looked at the flowers all wistfully like it was a waste for them to be pinned up like that.

But the real star of the fest, beyond the sugary sweets further down the street, was the gazebo. Twinkle lights around the roof and trees and street lights gave everything a soft glow. Then there were the hearts. Some were taped to benches and the small brick walls of the greenery. Some were pined to the leaves of the few scattered bushes and trees. And inside the gazebo was a shower of hearts. The little pieces of paper had been strung up, a few dozen to a string, and tied to the rafters of the gazebo. The effect was like walking through a field of sunflowers. Except pink.

Suddenly, Stephen's arm looped around mine and I was being walked/pulled towards the gazebo.

"Wait, what?"

"What? You wanna walk through the hearts, right?"

"I mean, if you want to. But they take pictures, so ..."

Stephen chuckled and kept walking us straight to the gazebo where Midge was taking pictures along with, who I assumed to be, the actual photographer Ms. Taylor hired for the event. He kept looking at her camera with a look I knew was trying to hold back correcting someone on something you're an expert at. I had the same feeling every time I saw the new car a friend got.

Seemingly unaware of the photographers, Stephen walked us up the steps and parted the first layer of hearts so I could step in. It was silly how much the little paper hearts enchanted me. But it really was gorgeous. It was the kind of pink, girlie moment my mom always wanted for me but I would refuse because I liked *boy* things. That was a stupid way of thinking in hindsight.

"Gorgeous," Stephen murmured, his phone out. Before I even had the chance to question what he was looking at, he turned the phone around. And on his screen was me, surrounded by blurred balls of pink and red, eyes bright as I looked around in wonderment. It was a pretty picture, taken with care. I was framed in the center, the focus.

I damn near jumped the man, the need to kiss him was just that bad. He'd done something so simple and my heart was doing flips. He made me feel again with so many little things. And a kiss was the only way I knew how to say thank you.

"Get a room!" Shea yelled and I pulled away from Stephen just enough to see Shea and the rest of my friends waving at us. Shea attempted the catcall whistle, only to make a harsh high-pitched noise that had Olivia covering her ears. Then, surprising everyone, Rosie let out a loud and clear whistle. Roxie damn near collapsed into Olivia as she laughed while Shea eagerly turned to beg Rosie to teach her.

"Your friends are ridiculous," Stephen murmured with a soft chuckle and the kind of tenderness that confirmed he meant it in a good way. "But I thought you said only couples could come? It looks like only Olivia has a date."

I stepped closer to him, settling under his arm and nudging his side. "It's not that you can't come with friends. But you can't bring somebody as a date if you're not *dating*."

"That seems like a superfluous distinction," he mumbled as we made our way through the curtain of hearts and down to my friends.

Shea almost had the cat whistle.

We paused at the bottom of the steps and Stephen looked at me, eyes slightly narrowed like he was looking for something specific. But whether he found what he was looking for or not, I couldn't tell. All he said before my friends rushed us was, "Good."

"The heart things a big deal." I waved my hand at the, probably, millions of hearts around us to emphasize my point. "You can't do it with just anyone."

21

SCRIBBLES AND TEARS

ZOEY

The festival was all blurry pink, bubbles in my chest, sugary sweets, and stupid jokes that made me laugh until I cried. I probably hadn't had as much fun at the Valentine's Fest since high school.

And it felt like I'd gotten the old me back. The me before heartbreak. And sure, some things had changed. But I was happy. The shadow wasn't hanging over my head and I wasn't on a constant low simmer.

Until I saw a recognizable tear amongst the hundreds of hearts pinned around downtown.

Then the storm was back. And it came back with a fucking vengeance.

I left the group with excuses of needing to go to the restroom and extra assurances that Stephen should just hang with my friends instead of awkwardly waiting outside the restroom for me. Then I headed straight to the torn heart.

I hadn't expected to see it tonight. I mean, what were the chances that I could find Johnny's and my heart amongst all the others? Especially the one from last year.

But there it was, tapped to the window of the pizza place. My handwriting, our names, the little tear on Johnny's side when he snatched the paper out of my hand because he was in a hurry for something. Maybe someone.

I tore the heart down and flipped it over.

On my side, I'd written *I hope you still love me next year.* I remember thinking he'd laugh at it and think I was being silly for doubting him.

Jokes on me, I guess.

Then I looked to Johnny's side to see what he'd written.

"I can't believe you actually brought that stranger here," a familiar voice said from behind me.

I turned around, my eyes too dry for any more tears, and held out the heart in front of Johnny's face. Then I tore it down the middle and let the scribble that should have been words of love fall to the ground. And stomped on it for good measure. Fuck him for ever making me think he loved me.

"I don't know why you're surprised." I twisted my foot, rubbing the scrap of paper into the ground. "He's my boyfriend and it's fucking Valentine's Day. That means something to some people."

Johnny rolled his eyes and scoffed, "You don't care about this crap. And I know he's not really you're boyfriend. Just some dumbass that can't drive straight and got caught up with your stupid revenge temper tantrum."

I crumpled and tossed the other half of the heart at him.

"Don't talk about Stephen like that," I gritted, hands balling into fists at my side.

"What? You actually care about that nerd? That's a first."

"A first? What the fuck do you mean by that?"

"You don't care about anything but your cars, Zo. That's all you've ever cared about. Until this new fucker apparently." People were starting to stare and I couldn't give a single fuck. I was too focused on resisting the urge to beat Johnny's ass.

"I care about him because he sees me as more than just my fucking hobby. He doesn't expect me to be somebody I'm not and he sure as hell doesn't tell me how to act like you have."

"Of course he hasn't. He's only known you for a week. Probably doesn't want to piss your crazy ass off."

"I. Am. Not. Crazy." I gritted each word. The crowd that I didn't care about seconds ago suddenly mattered. Because punching him or kicking him in the balls or anything else I wanted to do would prove him right. "Stephen knows me better than you ever did. And that's because he's done what you never did. He asks me questions, he asks about my friends, about my grief. He gives a shit about me. You only ever cared about me when I was acting the way you wanted me to."

"I never told you how to act. You're being dramatic," he scoffed. I threw up my hands, screaming at the sky.

"You didn't say the words exactly, sure. But if I talked about technical shit you didn't understand, you'd walk out of the room. If I so much as wore fucking lip gloss, you'd make a big production about how I didn't need to be like the other girls and complain about the taste. If I cursed too much or talked too loud because I was excited, you'd shush me. Do you know how fucking tiring that is? To keep track of all the ways you wanted me to behave and perform? And still feel like I was never doing enough?"

"Please. If you liked me enough to do all of that, you would've shown it."

"Showed it? Sorry if I was too tired after pretending all the time that I wasn't in the mood for sex." The whispers of the crowd around us escalated and it was only a matter of time before the girls or Stephen came by. And I really didn't want Stephen to be a part of this. I didn't want any more of my time with Stephen wasted on this asshole. Because that really was all he was anymore. A waste of time. "It doesn't matter. If you cared enough to have this conversation and listen to me, you would've done it before you slept around. See you at the race. Then hopefully never again."

I started walking away, keeping my pace even. I didn't want him to know how much damage he'd done, just by simply accusing me of not caring. I wanted to run though, run back to the people who made me feel comfortable cared for and like myself.

I should have run.

"Why don't we make it more interesting then?"

Like an idiot, I took the bait.

"You've caused me a shit ton of trouble, Zo. I'm one more fuck up away from losing my job."

"Sounds like the consequences of your actions. Sorry you don't like them."

"You plastered our business all over people's cars," he gritted. "I want the Miura."

I bit my tongue. The Miura was by far the most expensive car Dad left me. Estimated worth: a million dollars. Dad used to joke about it being my dowry. He'd gotten it in a steal from some family death garage sale. It'd been in shit condition, but it was one of the first cars we fixed up together. And we'd done a damn good job of it.

Johnny didn't give a damn about what that car meant to me or my dad. He just knew it was worth a lot.

That's all he ever wanted from me, my worth. Fuck if I'd let him have any more of it.

"Fine. But I get the GT."

22

RESEARCHING EFFICIENT AUTOMOTIVE LOGISTICS TO INFURIATE A ZEALOUS EGOTIST

ZOEY

Zoey was in her garage when I woke up again. I'd meandered out of our room to search for her in nothing but my sweats and when I found her, I stood at the garage door and watched. There was a slight chill in the air, but I couldn't tear myself away. This was the first time I got to watch Zoey work undisturbed, not because she was angry and hiding behind work, but because there was work to do and she was gonna get it done. And I wasn't going to miss a minute of it.

She'd braided her hair back, several strands loose and frizzy. Her jumpsuit was thankfully a different, black one, free of another man's hand prints, her logo bright on the back. And while dark goggles covered her eyes, I could tell she was focused on whatever it was she was working on. It was beautiful to watch her be so transfixed.

She didn't even notice I was there until an alarm on her phone went off.

"How long have you been watching me, weirdo?" she said once she'd turned off the alarm, hip cocked to the side.

"I don't know."

Zoey rested a hand on that hip and stared at me for a second. Then she rolled her eyes and tossed a dirty rag from her pocket at me.

"Such a weirdo," she mumbled, a small smirk spreading across her face. It was nice seeing her smile so often. It was how Zoey should always be, bright and happy.

She started to the house, but I wrapped an arm around her waist and pulled her into me. She smelled like engine oil and dust. And I must be truly gone for because that smell was actually doing it for me.

"Stephen," she half whined, half giggled. "I have to go to work."

"You're the boss though, so ..." I trailed off, pressing kisses to her neck. I didn't have high hopes of convincing her to stay. She ran a small business that relied on a storefront. But I did want to know if she was tempted.

Zoey tilted her head back against my shoulder to look at me. She'd scrunched up her face like she was trying to be stern but it just came off as cute. When she realized I was unaffected, she rolled her eyes, nudging her ass against my crotch before pushing away.

"It's nice having a sexual appetite again, but I *do* still need to make money. Stay here, you tempting little weirdo." She nudged me again, this time with her elbow and started to the house. I looked back to the garage and thought ...

"Is there anything I can do to help with the car?"

Zoey turned on her heel, pointing a finger at me. This time her stern look, set jaw and narrowed eyes, actually struck true.

"Don't you dare touch my car without me around," she gritted, taking slow steps towards me until her finger was right in my face.

I was tempted to bite it, but she moved it away before I could.

"Don't give me that look."

"What look?"

"You were gonna bite my finger because I wouldn't let you fuck with my car. Don't deny it, I could see it in your eyes."

"No," I said, as straightly as I could manage. "I was going to bite my finger because it's what you did to me."

"You don't get to do that, that's my thing."

"I don't think biting a finger can be *your thing*, Zoey."

"Well between the two of us, it is." Her alarm went off again and she threw her head back dramatically. "I have to go. Don't touch my car."

"Fine. But is there anything else I can do for you? Something that'll help with your race?"

Zoey paused, tilting her head and assessing me. I could see the comparisons running through her head. She was concentrating so hard and for so long, I was about to ask if she was attempting advanced calculus.

"Fine," she said, almost like she was surprised that that was where she landed. "You can change the tires. I need the ones marked with chalk on. All the supplies you'll need are in there and there are extra jumpsuits in the back closet." She paused again, hand on her hips. "You do know how to change a tire, right?"

"I think so," I answered honestly. Zoey exhaled, looked at her phone, and sighed again.

"Okay. Do your best, I guess. Shouldn't be too much trouble if you fuck up the tie," she grumbled, starting to walk away. But when she got to the door, she paused, then turned and rushed me. Zoey pressed a kiss to my cheek, murmured a goodbye, and then she was off.

It started when I put on one of the jumpsuits in the garage closet. One of Johnny's jumpsuits.

One of Johnny's jumpsuits that had a pair of panties in the pocket.

Panties that were certainly not Zoey's. Not her size, not her style. Not hers.

That fucker had come home with another woman's underwear in his pockets.

Everything after that realization was a blur.

I texted the girls' group chat asking where Johnny worked. Shea answered. I went.

His new job was as a cashier at a BBQ joint. The food smelt good, but seeing his face right upon entering ruined my appetite.

I heard him talk, but I didn't process any of the words he'd said. I was on autopilot. I had a mission.

And that mission was to punch this asshole and leave him with the burden of returning the panties.

So I did exactly that. I walked through the empty restaurant and up to the registrar. I balled my hand into a fist, pulled back my arm, and punched him. Then I dropped the panties on the counter and left.

I vaguely recalled hearing something about a 'last straw' as I left, but my head wasn't really cleared until I got back to Zoey's house and sank into the couch.

What the fuck did I just do? Why did I do that?

So I called Darren.

"Well look who finally decided —"

"I think I'm in love with Zoey."

There was a long pause, so long I actually pulled my phone away to check that the call hadn't disconnected.

But eventually, he sighed.

"Who's Zoey?"

"Darren," I grumbled. "Zoey, the mechanic I'm staying with and seeing."

"Seeing?" he repeated. "Since when?"

"Since the other day."

"And you love her?"

"Yes."

"Stephen, no."

"Darren, yes."

"You? Mr. Stoic, has a hard time keeping up with conversations, can barely manage to text me back to confirm you're alive, hyper-focuses on work so much you took it on vacation, is in love with a woman you've known for less than a month?" What Darren was saying made logical sense. I'd never been the type to fall in love quickly. But Zoey didn't follow logical sense, so why would falling in love with her follow it?

"I am. There's no other way to explain me nearly blacking out to punch her ex because I found another woman's panties in some clothes he left behind."

"You do recognize that that's a wild sentence for you to say and expect me to understand, right? The only thing you've told me about this girl is that she's cute and is the owner of the shop the car is at. And I only know that last part because you submitted a reimbursement receipt."

"Oh, right. I guess I've been ... distracted and haven't updated you on what's happened."

"No shit," Darren murmured. I chose to ignore the attitude and took a deep breath before recapping most of what had happened with Zoey and me over the past few days. I skimmed over the more intimate details, both the sexual and illegal activities. Those moments were for us and us alone.

Though knowing Zoey's friends, I doubt she'd be able to keep much from them. But I was fine with that. Not everything had to be exactly even.

"Well I'll be damned, you really are in love with her."

"What makes you say that? The fact that I went insane and punched a man?"

"No, the way you talk about her. You're smitten as fuck, my dude."

"What am I gonna do now? I told her I'd be able to do long distance, but I don't think I can do that anymore."

"Not yet," I murmured, though I should start a list of practical things I would need to get done because I couldn't leave. I didn't want to. But ... "How do I ask her if I can stay? How do I tell her I love her?"

"Ha, knowing you, you've already looked into how to get the car back without having to do it yourself."

"I dunno, but she sounds just as crazy as you are, so I'm sure it'll go fine. Just don't forget to invite me to the wedding."

"I think it's a little too early to be talking about *that*." Although the suggestion called to mind a clear image of Zoey on that gazebo in long, flowing lace. I wonder if the town council or whoever ran the festivals would let us use the hearts for a gazebo wedding.

"You're totally thinking about it now though." I grumbled and Darren went on, "If I had known I'd never see my best friend again, I might not have pushed you to take that vacation."

"You're being dramatic. I'll come back to Seattle for business meetings."

"Business meetings, he says. Dramatic, he says. As if I'm the one moving across the country for a woman I'd only known for a few weeks."

"Do you know anything about cars?" I asked, hoping to derail his dramatics with more useful conversation.

"I mean ... what kind of cars?"

23

SOME MEN DESERVE BLOWJOBS

ZOEY

Shea: So this is maybe, technically, a little bit my fault

Roxie: It's one hundred percent your fault

Rosie: Oh dear, what did he do after that text?

Me: What are y'all talking about?

Shea: Stephen asked us where Johnny worked and, like, he seemed to have a reasonable head on his shoulders, so I didn't think he'd do anything bad with that info

Me: I find it very weird that y'all have a group chat with Stephen. Did y'all ever have a chat with Johnny?

Shea: But apparently he went and got Johnny fired

Roxie: By going in and punching that bitch right in the face! Then dropping some panties on the counter

Roxie: Sorry Zo, but I do think it's important to know he did that because of finding those and not because he was doing some stupid possessive claiming thing

Rosie: I don't know, a little possessiveness is nice

Shea: All right, Rosie, wanna tell us what else you're into?

Roxie: I'll keep an eye out for you.

Rosie: Oh hush, you two. I was just saying it's not an immediate red flag

Roxie: For you

Shea: No, I get what she's saying. I think if some girl went out of their way to defend my honor or some shit, I'd swoon

Ashley: Ew, if I ever let a man take some sort of possessive claim over me, check me into a mental hospital

Ashley: Where is the closest facility?

Roxie: I'm not sure, actually. But hard same

Bailey: I never would have expected to wake up to such a polarizing conversation

Rosie: Wake up? Dear, it's 2:00 p.m.

Bailey: Had a gallery last night, a little wine, a little flirt

Roxie: Oooo, a flirt with whom?

Shea: Excuse me? Why is this the first I'm hearing of this?

Bailey: It's just some guy that likes my photography, big art donor, rich guy. It's probably nothing

Shea: Uh-huh and where'd you sleep last night?

Olivia: We can talk about Bailey's dalliances later.

Olivia: Zoey, how do you feel about what Stephen did?

Me: I'm gonna close the shop early and let him know

Roxie: GET IT!

One of the better things about owning the only auto shop in town was that taking off one day didn't matter much because if somebody needed to come by when I randomly decided to close shop to go suck off my boyfriend, most folks would rather wait a day than go out of their way to go to the next closest shop.

Was it irresponsible? Possibly. But fuck if I could just sit around the shop doing stupid admin work when Stephen got all unhinged for me. When he'd gotten so mad on my behalf he actively sought out the wrongdoer. And sure, it stung knowing he'd somehow found evidence of Johnny's cheating *at* my house, but the anger that inspired was comforted by Stephen's actions.

And I had to reward that, right?

So I went home. I dropped my shit on the floor, walked straight through the house, and found him in the garage.

And fuck, I didn't realize this cute little dork would look so hot working on my car. His hair had been pushed back so much, it looked gelled back. There was a streak of black across his forehead where he probably wiped away some sweat. And he'd taken off the top half of his jumpsuit, tying the arms around his waist like I always did.

I didn't even care that he'd clearly been fucking with shit under the hood, I was so turned on.

Leaning against the door, I watched him for a bit. He's movements were clumsy, but he had a notebook that he kept referencing, so I figured he had a plan and knew what he was doing. At least to a certain extent. He did have a sketch on that notebook that was upside down for a solid minute or two.

"Hey, Stephen," I finally said once I'd had my fill of watching him. Stephen jerked in surprise, nearly knocking his head on the hood. When he turned to face me, his eyes were wide with worry, like a kid caught with his hand in the cookie jar.

"How long have you been watching me, weirdo?" he said, a little sheepish as he repeated my words from earlier.

"I don't know." I copied his response, though the answer was true. Watching him fumble through whatever it was he was trying to do was endearing.

But I was done with endearing.

I took a few steps to Stephen, grabbing the sleeves tied at his waist and yanking him to me.

"I heard about what happened at Cheekys." I looked up into his eyes, catching him steeling himself for my reaction. "You got him fired."

"I found —" he started but I put a finger to his lip, raising one brow in a challenge. Instead of biting my finger, he pursed his lips, pressing a short kiss to the tip of my finger. "It's not gonna cause you any trouble, is it?"

"Hmm, I don't think I care if it does," I murmured as I pulled the sleeves loose, keeping eye contact with him as I sank to my knees. "In fact, I think you deserve a reward for your actions."

I ran my palm over him, his cock hardening under my touch. After a few more passes, I moved my fingers to the zipper and waited.

"Fuck," he whispered. One hand went behind him, bracing himself on the edge of the car, and the other slid down my face to grip my chin. "I don't think punching an asshole is worth this. But I can't fucking say no."

"I don't want you to," I whispered back before slowly dragging the zipper down. The hiss of the metal pulling apart sent a hot thrill through me. There wasn't a single part of this moment that felt performative. It was all real, the want, the heat, the way drool pooled in my mouth.

When the zipper reached his knees, I yanked the fabric down and Stephen kicked his legs free. Even with the movement, his eyes didn't leave mine. Not until I pulled down his boxers to free his cock and they rolled back.

"I haven't even touched you yet and you're struggling to keep your eyes open," I teased, situating myself closer to him while I ran my hands over his thighs.

"You do a number on me, pretty girl. It's hard to see straight." The hand on my chin let go to comb my hair away from my face, fingers tightening there. I hummed in response before trailing my tongue over the head of his cock. After spending a moment tracing the split of his head and relishing the way he shook in response, I slid my lips over him and down his shaft until I damn near couldn't breathe.

He tasted amazing, even as he suffocated me. He had that salty taste of a man who had been working hard. Work he'd been doing *for* me. That thought alone was enough to make me wet for him. Having his cock in my mouth, wrapping a hand around him to massage what I couldn't take, it all reminded me of how fucking good he felt inside me too. By the time I was ready to really work him with my mouth, I was dripping.

As Stephen's hand tightened in my hair, I started sucking harder, twisting my hand up and down. Each moan and grunt and whimper sped me on. It was intoxicating, watching my dorky weirdo melt from sexual pleasure at my hands.

"Have mercy on me, pretty girl. Please."

I pulled back just enough so that the head of his cock rested on my lips, my breath tickling the swollen skin. "What do you mean?"

"Let me take you to bed. I can't take much more of this." His voice was ragged and the hand in my hair twitched.

I slid my mouth back over his cock.

"Zoey," he groaned, pulling ever so gently at my hair. It was nice how gentle he was, even on the brink of coming in my mouth.

But this was his reward, after all, so I should give him what he wants.

"All right." I pulled away from his cock and took his hand from my hair to pull myself up. "Let me take you to bed."

Keeping my hand in his, I dragged us through the backyard, despite Stephen's concerns about being half naked, and into the house. Once inside, I dropped his hand and ran to my room, tossing off my clothes as I went. I heard Stephen grumble something behind me before his shirt hit the back of my head.

"Hey, no fair," I shouted back at him before ducking into my room to avoid his boxers.

When Stephen rounded the doorway, his eyes were dark as he growled, "I thought this was my reward."

"It is, I was just fooling around." I leaned over the bed to pull the sheets down and as I stretched over, Stephen yanked off my last remaining clothes and grinded his hard cock against my ass.

"Yeah, and this is what you're fooling around does to me, naughty." He grinded against me again, rougher. But when I tilted my hips so he could push in, he pulled back. "Fuck, I —you could light a car on fire and I'd have a hard-on."

I flipped onto my back, since he clearly wasn't about to fuck me, and grabbed his hand to pull him onto the bed.

"I would never do that," I said as I straddled him. Hands on his shoulders, I pushed him back to lie down on the bed. His hands went to my ass, gripping hard enough to leave marks. "Burning a car would be a waste. And dangerous." Lifting my hips, I rested my cunt on his cock, grinding my clit over him.

"Fuck," he hissed. "I'd still hand you the matches. Whatever you want pretty girl, whatever I need to do to keep you." His hands on my waist began to pull me, grinding me faster.

"I thought you were against illegal activities," I teased, but my voice cracked with pleasure. I might come from just rubbing against his cock. "What changed?"

"I ... god, just come for me, pretty girl." His left hand let go of my hip to twist into my hair and pull me down for a searing kiss. His tongue ran over mine with such thoroughness I thought he must be memorizing every piece of me. And I returned that energy, needing to know every inch of him just as badly. Especially the hard inches that twitched with each pass of my cunt. The friction, his hand on my hip, the grip in my hair, his *fucking* tongue. It tore me apart.

Were orgasms supposed to be this intense every time?

Because holy fuck, did I see stars. I couldn't keep my eyes open as my body fought between not being able to keep moving and desperately wanting more.

When I managed to open my eyes, my sight went straight to the little scratches across Stephen's shoulders. Marks of where I abandoned sense in my orgasm. Marks that showed where I held onto as my body lost control.

Stephen let go of my hair, hand trailing down my arm until our fingers met over the scratches. He traced the irritated skin before entwining our fingers.

"Scratch me up some more, Zoey. I like it. It lets me know how you're feeling."

"How will I know how you're feeling?" I asked, not recognizing my own voice from how breathy it was.

"That's simple. If it's you doing it, I love it."

Before I had the opportunity to process those words, to swoon over them if I'm being honest, he was tilting my hips to slam into me. And fuck, I couldn't think while full of his cock. It was all I could do to collapse onto his chest and hold on as he bucked into me.

Stephen's hands went to my ass, bouncing me at a speed that had me muffling my screams into his neck. It was too much. It was perfect. And when he readjusted so his pelvis gave my clit the attention it needed, I came again, screaming his name, scratching his shoulders.

This time, he allowed me a real breather. Though I could feel his cock twitching inside me, aching for its turn.

So I pushed up, hands on his chest, and resituated myself onto my feet. Stephen hissed out a curse before pushing himself up, hand propping him up from behind, his shoulders back in reach to help me keep balance. Which was good because with the way his cock was hitting me at this angle and the remaining shakes from that last orgasm, it was a struggle to keep my head up. But after a few bounces on his cock, I caught my rhythm.

"Come for me, Stephen," I whispered and the man shook his head.

"No. You first. We made a deal. Three times." His breath was so ragged, his Adam's apple bobbing. He was holding on for dear life because of a stupid thing I'd said just to get him to fuck me quicker.

Why was that so damn endearing?

"Then make me," I whispered the words, leaning close enough so our lips grazed. His arms jerked, straining to push closer so he could kiss me. It was a desperate kiss, wet and sloppy, teeth scraping lips and tongues dragging across each other roughly. It made me feel alive. It reminded me of the different kinds of heat my body could feel. The best kind of heat, not from anger or frustration or embarrassment, but out of … pleasure wasn't the right word, maybe affection?

The word didn't matter so much as the feeling of coming with him. Like an intense sigh of relief. Like warming up from being out in the cold.

His arms wrapped around me, holding me tight as we collapsed onto the bed. We lay there, sweaty and out of breath. Twenty-eight years old and this was the first time I understood wanting to fall asleep, cuddled up with someone after sex.

"Don't fall asleep on me yet, pretty girl," Stephen murmured, one hand rubbing circles across my back.

"Hmm, why not? I closed the shop, might as well take a nap."

"How can you close your shop so often without worrying about money?"

"Oh, I'm a billionaire. Didn't you know?" I half-heartedly waved my hand around the room as if my wealth was reflected in the cottage aesthetic of my house.

"Mhmm. And what is it you spend your billions on?"

"Cars. Car storage. Car parts." I shrugged and Stephen jerked up, sitting us both upright. He stared at me for a solid minute, hands held together at my lower back.

"*Are* you a billionaire? When you include all your assets?"

I nearly fell back laughing.

"No, Stephen, I'm not a billionaire," I said through snorting laughter. Stephen hummed in disbelief before jerking us to standing. I wrapped my legs around him and let him carry me out of the room. I didn't have to ask where he was taking me. I'd asked him to clean me up once and Stephen wasn't the kind of man to forget those sorts of requests.

"So none of those cars you've got stored god knows where are worth that much?"

"One or two might be. But I wouldn't sell them for anything." I shrugged and Stephen gave me one quick squeeze.

"Your dad's?" he asked. Forget about requests, Stephen was the kind of man who *remembered*. It didn't matter what it was, he remembered.

"Yeah, they're my dad's."

24

Points Against Recklessly Terrorizing Yahoos

Stephen

This time when Zoey was suddenly called out by her friends, I was invited too.

I hadn't felt excluded by their last night out, normally I'd be happy to do my own thing at home instead of being social. But being included felt like a mark of acceptance. Like her friends trusted me and supported my relationship with Zoey. And knowing how much her friends meant to her, how much they all cared for each other, made the inclusion all the more valuable.

When we entered Rosie's diner, the backmost table erupted to welcome us before quickly returning to whatever they were doing. Shea was messing with the jukebox with Roxie over her shoulder and Dennis and Olivia were cuddled in the booth talking with Rosie, a phone propped up on the napkin holder between them. Ashley was missing, but that seemed to be a common occurrence given her job.

Zoey dragged me over to the table, a bounce in her step, and we settled in next to Rosie. Close up, I could see the phone was on a video call with Bailey, a woman who looked like she was vegan and did yoga. I can't exactly describe *why* that was my first impression of her, but it was.

"Pssst," Zoey whispered, leaning into me after hugging Rosie. "Did you just think that Bailey looks like a hippie?"

My brow instantly furrowed. Had I really been that obvious? Or was Zoey just able to read me better now?

"I didn't think she was a hippie."

"Mhmm. But?" Zoey asked, elbowing my side.

"But I did consider if she was vegan and did yoga," I conceded.

"That tracks. She's not a vegan, though I do think she did yoga for a while. I remember her complaining about this one dude in class who just kept making obnoxious noises. Like grunts and shit."

"That was in pilates!" Bailey chimed in. "Like I get the class is hard, but everybody else manages to keep the noise to the minimum. It's only ever dudes that make noise."

"I still think that's a little judgmental, dear," Rosie started, only to be immediately interrupted by the front door of the restaurant being slammed open, the bell over it vibrating angrily.

At the door, was Ashley, looking ... exasperated. She took slow steps towards us, ignoring the waitress who greeted her as she came in, her slippers slapping on the black and white vinyl. She sank into the booth next to me, eyes full of murder. Roxie and Shea instantly sat down on the other side of the booth, eager to hear what brought Ashley out here so late in the day.

"He ordered a fucking mariachi band to 'serenade' me. Told them if I didn't respond right away, it was because I was wearing headphones, so they just needed to be louder." Ashley threw her arms around as she spoke and I had to duck to keep from getting smacked in the face.

Across the table, Shea sank into her seat, biting her lips, clearly trying not to laugh. Roxie on the other hand smirked as she grabbed a fry from one of the baskets of food scattered across the table.

"Serenade, huh? Interesting word choice," she murmured as she dragged the fry through some ketchup and took a bite. The other woman simply glared in response.

"Were they, like, in the whole outfit?" Shea said between snickers, half her face blocked by the table. Dennis started chuckling too and Olivia elbowed him.

"It's not funny. He knew she was in bed," Olivia argued. She seemed to be the only one on Ashley's side though.

"It is sort of romantic though," Rosie sighed.

"What song did they sing?" Bailey asked.

"I have no fucking clue. I don't speak Spanish and I don't give a damn what he paid them to sing," she muttered.

"Did it go like this?" Bailey asked before proceeding to sing in, what seemed to be, perfect Spanish.

"This is revenge for you trashing his apartment the other week," Roxie pointed out and Rosie's eyes went wide at the memory as she nodded her head.

"I didn't 'trash' his apartment. I just messed with a few things. Nothing worth ruining my sleep for."

"Didn't you cut the chord to his alarm clock?" Shea asked, still half laughing under the table.

"Sure, but who actually uses their alarm clock these days when we have phones?"

Rosie, Shea, and Olivia held up their hands.

"Seriously?" Ashley shouted, mouth agape. I was surprised too, especially since Zoey uses her phone alarms to an aggressive level.

Rosie made a pointed look at the waitress manning the counter and gave her some complicated hand signs. Meanwhile, the rest of the girls argued over the use of alarm clocks and if Mason hiring a mariachi band was 'too much'. It was at the height of the argument that the waitress set several milkshakes on the table and all the girls happily quieted to enjoy their dessert.

happily quieted to enjoy their dessert. While everyone was drinking, Olivia gave me a look and pointed her head to the side. When I nodded, she quickly pecked Dennis on the cheek and then tapped on Shea to get her and Roxie to move out of her way. I copied her movements, a kiss for Zoey and a tap for Ashley. Not a single beat of the conversation, which had turned Bailey's remarkable Spanish, was missed as we moved around.

I followed Olivia around the corner of the diner and we sat at the counter, out of sight of the others. For a long moment, nothing was said. Olivia's face twisted as she rearranged the sugar packets on the counter. a nervous habit.

I waited until she was ready to say whatever it was that was bothering her. Bracing for the possibility that she didn't approve of how my relationship with Zoey was progressing. I couldn't exactly blame her for being concerned. But —

"Do you think you could talk Zoey out of doing the race?"

"Oh." That's not what I was expecting. But at least the answer to that question was simple. "No."

Olivia threw her head back and groaned.

"She won't tell us where this race is, what sort of track it is, the safety precautions. When I asked if there were paramedics on site, she stared at me like I was an idiot. I know she's a good mechanic and can make a safe, fast car or whatever. But racing is different! She's never raced before, did she tell you that?"

Olivia paused just long enough for me to think she wanted a response, but when I opened my mouth to say something, she started talking again.

"Anytime we've gone on a trip together, she's not allowed to drive. She speeds like crazy. I swear, if she lived in a city where you had to get on the interstate regularly, she'd rack up speeding tickets like a ... like ... I don't know, really fucking quickly."

Another pause. This time I didn't try to speak.

"And just going fast isn't going to be enough for her to win against Johnny. It especially won't keep her safe if Johnny tries to do anything dirty. I mean — she never brought us to whatever these drag race things are. For all I know, they could be adult bumper caring each other around a track. And she's sure as fuck pissed Johnny off enough for him to try something. What if he cuts her breaks before the race? Or just slams into her door? How will we know that she's not just dead in a ditch somewhere? All because she went a little overboard arguing one night."

"I'll let you know how the race goes and confirm she isn't dead in a ditch," I assured but when her head whipped to face me, I knew that was the wrong move.

"You get to go?" she screeched before jumping out of her seat and rushing back over to everyone else. Before I even had the chance to get off the stool, I heard her question, "How come Stephen gets to go?"

"Stephen!" Zoey shouted and I quickened my steps to rejoin the group. "Why'd you tell her?"

Zoey looked at me like it should have been obvious to hide something from her best friend. Once again, Zoey had no trouble reading my thoughts and rolled her eyes in response.

"Okay, fine. But like, why'd it even come up?"

"She's worried about you. I told her I'd let her know you're okay."

"What're you worried for?" Zoey asked, turning to Olivia.

"What am I worried for? Zo, you drive like a maniac!"

"You're exaggerating. Just because I like to speed a little, doesn't mean I drive like a maniac."

"A little?" Shea, Olivia, and I said in unison, all at varying degrees of disbelief.

"Okay, fine. So I speed. So what?"

"So it's unsafe," Olivia argued. "And for whatever reason, you're gonna let *Stephen* go, but not us? No offense, Stephen."

"None taken," I murmured while Zoey just shrugged.

"He helped me with the car, so I figured it's only fair."

"Woah, she let you help with the car?" Shea said in a soft whisper. When I nodded, the girls went still.

"Zoey, you gonna tell us before you marry the man at least? Because that might as well be a proposal coming from you," Shea joked. Zoey rolled her eyes and Dennis chuckled a little, but everybody else turned to look at Olivia. She was looking at her best friend, eyes watery.

"O, darling," Dennis started, pushing up to his feet. Shea and Roxie quickly moved to let him out but Olivia was faster. She was out the door before Dennis had a chance to shout her name ... letter, again.

Dennis stood in the walkway of the diner, dropped his back, and groaned. Then he turned back to point at Zoey.

"She's just worried about you, Zoey. You're doing a shit ton of reckless bullshit with a stranger over her. The least you could do is acknowledge that shit hurts her feelings." Dennis snatched Olivia's bag and jacket that Shea held up for him and marched out. A part of me wanted to step in and defend Zoey. But ... I could see it, the hurt in Olivia's face when she realized there were parts of Zoey she didn't get to see or help. I couldn't think of an exact instance, but I'm sure I've hurt Darren the same way. And maybe me and Zoey being similar in that way meant we could help each other when our heads were up our asses.

"I think you should go talk to her." I could feel all eyes turn to look at me, but I concentrated on Zoey and how her eyes narrowed.

"You too?"

"She pulled me aside just to see if I could convince you not to race. She's worried about you. That's what best friends do. Even if it's annoying and inconvenient sometimes."

For a beat, Zoey just stared at me while the others stared at us. I could feel them fight to keep quiet, to keep from pushing Zoey any further, but I knew she didn't need it. Zoey knew what she needed to do, she just also needed a second to be stubborn about it.

"Yeah, all right. I'll go talk to her."

25

TALKING ABOUT FEELINGS STILL FUCKING SUCKS

ZOEY

By the time I walked down the downtown strip and found Olivia at the gazebo, my head had cooled off just enough to not be bitter that Stephen and Dennis were right.

I've been a shitty friend.

And maybe I had a hard time reacting to any sort of criticism about it.

So when I got into sight of Dennis and Olivia, I didn't blame Dennis for stepping in front of her. But Olivia tugged on his pant leg, gave him a look, and off he went. Though not before giving me a strong look that said 'I can't do anything to you because my girl loves you, but that doesn't mean you can keep being a dick'.

I guess I could respect that.

Once Dennis had walked away, I took the spot next to Olivia on the gazebo steps. We didn't say anything for a long while. I'm pretty sure Olivia was avoiding looking at me, determined that I had to be the one to speak first. Which was fine by me. I just needed to figure out *how* to say what I needed to.

"Stephen seems nice, I guess," Olivia grumbled before I could put together what to say. "But I don't think he should get to help you with your car and not me."

"Ma'am, last time I let you help, you accidentally stabbed the windshield wiper fluid container."

"That was in high school," she argued, speaking into her knees she'd pulled up and wrapped her arms around. I nudged her with my whole body, and just leaned right into her for that lame-ass argument. She might've worked at the shop for a couple of years but I never let her touch the cars, for good reason.

"I didn't really let Stephen help if that makes you feel any better. I mean, I said he could change the tires because it seemed like if I left him alone, he'd do a lot of other shit. But he did that anyways because he felt guilty over the whole getting Johnny fired thing." Olivia made some sort of grumbled response and I took a deep breath and said what I didn't want to admit.

"It's embarrassing, you know? To be the girl that got cheated on. To be so disrespected by someone I chose to put my faith in. For it to become public knowledge because he wrecked my fucking Corvette getting a goddamn blowjob. And then, you know, I haven't exactly reacted well. I'm not proud of TP-ing that asshole's cousin's house or stealing his car. Even if he does deserve all that shit, what does it say about me that I sank to that level? I'm ... ashamed of all doing all that shit. Especially since it didn't even make me feel better. And telling you guys is embarrassing and the idea of dragging you into it, having you watch me be an unhinged piece of shit, makes me want to lock myself in the garage forever.

"As for Stephen ... I dunno. He was just there and nice and I didn't care that he saw me become an unhinged monster because I was just using him to get under Johnny's skin. But then he just *kept* being nice about all my shit and I guess that made me trust him with it.

"So ... you know, I'm sorry for not telling you or involving you in my shit. I was embarrassed about it or whatever. And Stephen isn't replacing you or anything, he's just a nice guy who happens to have an uncanny ability to make me talk about my feelings. He's also got a nice dick. So there's really no comparing you two."

Olivia threw herself at me, arms wrapping tight around my shoulder. When I regained my balance from the force of her hug, I squeezed her back.

"Why the fuck would you be embarrassed about all that when I was living with my parents until a few months ago?" she said, voice shaky like she was about to cry. That kinda made my eyes tear up a little bit too.

"You know I didn't give a shit about that."

"Yeah, well you should know I don't give a shit about how crazy you get."

I pulled back and gave her the 'that's bullshit' look.

"Uh-huh, and did knowing I loved you despite where you were living help you feel any less bad about it? Because I remember having several pep talks about how it didn't matter."

Olivia let go of me with a little shove and rolled her eyes.

"Fine, I'll admit it's hard to get out of your own head about that kind of shit."

"It's so fucking stupid," I murmured, kicking at a small pebble on the walkway.

"Are you really gonna do the race?" Olivia asked quietly.

"Oh absolute. There's not a chance in hell you could convince me not to. That bastard needs to eat my dust." Then, because I figured I owed Olivia some secrets, I added, "Plus I sorta bet my Miura on it."

"You what?" Olivia shouted and smacked my arm. "What the fuck were you thinking? That car's like you're fucking retirement fund."

"Well I'm not gonna lose, so it's not a problem. And I haven't told Stephen, so don't mention anything about it in that little group chat of yours."

"Oh my god," Olivia murmured, hiding her head in her hands.

"Don't worry. I'll win. Johnny's an idiot and relies too much on catching up during turns."

"It's not like a NASCAR thing is it? You don't run into each other, right?"

"Is that what you've been thinking it was this whole time?" I asked through a laugh.

"Well, what else was I supposed to think? You made it sound like some sort of illegal racing."

"I mean, it is illegal. But like, it's also just a dirt track on some abandoned farmland. They just race in circles. Faster than you legal should go."

"God," she whispered. She opened her mouth to say something but the sound of steps stopped her.

Our men stepped into view with the sort of awkward tension that could only mean they'd walked over here together and had no clue what to say to each other. The picture of the two of them struggling to come up with small talk, knowing their girls were close so they should be too, and just failing miserably since neither of them were good at small talk, made me giggle.

"You good, O?" Dennis asked, head tilted as he examined her. Olivia nodded, wiping her eyes and giving me a quick hug before hopping up and taking Dennis' hand. While they walked off, Stephen took up the seat beside me.

"This is where you spread your dad's ashes, right?" Stephen asked after a short silence. I looked over at him, almost suspicious that he managed to remember what I'd said about my dad and bothered to bring it back up. But I guess I shouldn't be surprised by that sort of thing anymore.

"Yeah, this is dear old Dad's resting place." I patted the railing of the gazebo, a little nostalgic for the days when I was a kid on my dad's shoulders without a single clue what heartbreak felt like.

Beside me, Stephen stood and then turned to face the gazebo.

"Hello, Mr. Riggs. Sorry we didn't have a chance to speak last time we were here. I was a little distracted." He looked at the roof of the gazebo, then at me, a soft smile lighting up his face. "She was just so pretty surrounded by pink."

I nudged his leg with my foot, leaving a bit of dirt on his jeans.

"Are you seriously telling my Dad's not-grave how you think I'm pretty?"

"I think he'd like to know," he told me before looking up again. "I imagine you and Johnny were pretty close and you must be … well if you're anything like Zoey, you're probably feeling a little murderous." That got a chuckle out of me. Dad wasn't the 'clean your shotgun when somebody picks up your daughter' kind of dad, but he sure as hell would've been making threats had he known what Johnny'd done.

"But you've got nothing to worry about, sir. Zoey's handling things. And I — oh, sorry, sir. I'm Stephen Gill, your daughter's new boyfriend. I don't know much about cars, but I love to listen to your daughter talk about them."

"God, you're so corny. Are you almost done, weirdo?" I asked, fighting a grin.

"Just one more thing," he said, looking away from me while he spoke. "I promise to help her beat that asshole tomorrow. And with anything else she needs. For as long as she'll have me."

With that last line, he looked back at me, holding out a hand. I took it and let him pull me up before saying, "Such a weirdo."

"You've said that before," Stephen noted.

"Yeah well, Dad would've called you one too. So I've gotta make up for his absence." Stephen wrapped an arm around my waist and I snuggled into his side. Dad would've loved Stephen, especially the lack of small talk. He would've made fun of the way Stephen stays quiet. He would've been aghast at his car choices and given him a lecture on finding a better one. He would've been thrilled to have Stephen on the trivia team. And whenever Stephen left and we were alone, he would've assured me that I was much better off with Stephen, even if he had shit knowledge of cars.

"He would've liked you," I whispered, needing to say that aloud so the knowledge didn't sit uncomfortably in my chest. In return, Stephen kissed my forehead.

"Good to know. Make sure you tell your mom that, might make me less nervous when we finally get to meet."

26

ZOOM ZOOM MOTHER FUCKERS

ZOEY

I was fine all throughout the workday. I was fine when I got home. I was even fine when I secretly switched out some of the work Stephen had. But on the way to the race, my knees bounced uncontrollably.

"What part of this is making you most nervous, pretty girl?" Stephen asked, his hand stilling my knee.

"Seeing everybody." The answer came so easily once Stephen asked, it was unfair.

"Who constitutes everybody?"

"All the folks I'd normally see at these things. A lot of them don't fix up their own cars and the ones that do prefer newer models, so we never crossed paths at any other car events I go to. Plus most of them aren't from Snowfall. So they were race friends, they were Johnny's and my friends. There wasn't really a clear divide until ..."

"He fucked one of them?"

I snorted, then smacked Stephen's arm.

"Don't make me laugh while I'm driving."

"Do you think they'll be mean to you or something?"

"No, I just ..." I paused to think and Stephen didn't push me for an answer. Even when it took me until we parked by the farm to figure it out.

"They only knew the person I was around Johnny and that person's dead. I don't think they were ever really alive to begin with. So now I'm basically a stranger to them and I don't know how to navigate that. I mean, it's not like I was a *totally* different person, but it's a noticeable difference. So it's gonna be all awkward with them on top of all the bullshit with Johnny and his band of dumbasses."

"Do you want to stay friends with them?"

"Ah, I dunno. I don't imagine I'm coming back here after tonight. It's stupid that it's bothering me. I don't think I'd stay friends with any of them if I just moved or something, it's just weird for it to ... stop so definitively, for me to go out there knowing this is the last time I'll talk to these perfectly fine people. Is it weird that I care about that?"

"I don't think so," Stephen said, though there was a bit of an uncertain quiver to his voice.

"Very convincing," I murmured.

"Zoey, I feel weird in nearly every social situation that doesn't involve you or Darren. So it sounds normal to me, but I don't think I'm the best judge." Stephen shrugged and I leaned over to kiss his cheek.

"Thanks, weirdo. I feel better now." I squeeze Stephen's hand once before killing the engine and stepping out into the growing crowd of drag racers.

The second I was out of the car, I was bombarded by questions. Where had I been, why didn't I ride with Johnny, who was the dude I brought, what kinda work did I get done on my car, why did Johnny's car make a funky noise last race, was this my first race tonight?

All their questions made one thing clear. None of them had a clue what Johnny had done. And I might be healing from the breakup or whatever, but I was still a petty bitch.

"Johnny and I aren't together anymore, he cheated on me." It was a simple recap of what had happened. It left out the important detail of my poor, ruined Corvette. But for the first time, those simple words didn't sting. And that felt better than any of the dumb shit I did to Johnny over the past month.

That feeling of unbotheredness lasted all of five minutes when *that* girl stepped into view. The rest of the folks had started dispersing and gossiping amongst themselves, so Stephen was the only one to notice my shift in attitude. Him and the girl, who was walking straight to me.

"Zoey, can we talk for a —" she started, but Stephen stepped in front of me before she could finish the question.

"No," was all Stephen said to make the girl shrink in place. Her eyes widened a fraction before she nodded and walked off.

And for some unknown reason, I followed her.

Or maybe I did know. The shame in her eyes was too familiar to ignore.

So I followed her, grabbed her arm, and said, "It's not gonna make me feel any better, but go ahead and say it."

The woman was silent for a moment. I let go of her arm and gave her some space to collect her thoughts or whatever. I imagined it wasn't easy for her to approach me, so I'd give her some grace. Some.

"I'm sorry. He'd told me y'all had broken up early last year and —"

"But I've been here since then. *With* him." I might be willing to let her say her apology, but I certainly wasn't gonna stay quiet during it. Or let either of them get away with some dumbass leaps in logic to justify what they'd done.

"I know ... I know. He said y'all were still friends and that we'd avoid PDA here just to keep things less awkward for everyone."

"Wow. That's some malevolent, manipulative bullshit."

"You guys never kissed or anything, even when he won. So I —"

"I don't care," I interrupted because I had a feeling she'd run through a long ass list of dumb, tiny reasons why she believed that asshole's lies. I didn't want to hear them. Especially since they'd all be signs that my relationship was falling apart before I noticed it. "You can take him or leave him. I really don't fucking care. All I want —"

The rev of an engine and the squeal of tires caught everyone's attention as Johnny stopped the fucking GT in the middle of the parking area. Taking up so much space and shouting and causing a general ruckus as he stepped out with his cousin. He flashed everyone with a bright smile, immediately talking about the car and how he was gonna win the race before anyone could get another word in.

"All I want is to beat that asshole."

I pushed through the crowd until I was face to face with Johnny. His eyes narrowed at me and I struggled to remember a time when I looked into those eyes and saw love.

"Ready to race, mother fucker?"

27

RATTLING ANXIETY CAUSES EXHAUSTION

STEPHEN

The ruckus that started when Zoey said mother fucker was wild and incomprehensible. There was hollering, engine revving, beer cans popping, and just loud chaos. And Zoey was the center of it.

Folks surrounded her, patted her on the back, whispered things that made her laugh, pointed out something on Johnny's car and nodded seriously. Zoey might've been nervous about tonight for several reasons, but these people shouldn't have been one of her concerns. They might not be her people in the way that her girls were, but they were still friendly.

One man even tried to pull me into conversation, asking where I was from and how I met Zoey. And when I told him I wasn't a fan of small talk, he nodded, murmured 'respect' and walked off.

After a while, the chatter died and folks started clearing the area in favor of some benches set up by the dirt track. I rejoined Zoey at her car, rounding the vehicle as she talked to Johnny's cousin, checking for any sort of defects and keeping myself occupied. But of course, there wasn't anything left to check for. Zoey had spent several hours on the car last night and this morning. There's nothing she would've missed that I would catch. But nerves were catching up to me and I was suddenly very concerned about everything Olivia had brought up yesterday.

I was relieved when Zoey finally opened her car door and I could be in a secluded space with her again.

"What're you doing, Stephen?" Zoey asked when I got into the car, hand frozen on the seat belt.

"What do you mean?"

"What do I — you can't ride with me through a race."

"Why not?"

"Why not? It's dangerous, Stephen," Zoey shouted as if I had no sense.

"If it's so dangerous that you can't have a passenger, then maybe you shouldn't do this."

"Oh my god, Olivia's anxiety is contagious, I swear," she grumbled, knocking her head on the steering wheel twice. "It's not dangerous because the racing is dangerous. It's dangerous because you being here is a distraction."

"What if I promise not to distract you, pretty girl?" I asked, the endearment just sort of slipping out accidentally. Apparently, that was the wrong thing to say.

"Get out of here," she said, smacking my arm. I sighed but started getting out. Until Zoey grabbed my arm. "Wait."

She pulled me to her and our lips met. A soft kiss, a quick graze of tongues.

"New tradition," she said. "You kiss me when you get nervous."

"You're going to have to travel some for that to work, I get nervous before meetings," I noted. Zoey hummed and kissed me again before giving me a little shove to the door.

"We'll figure that out later."

I got out of the car and as soon as I stepped away, Zoey revved her engine. She made a sharp turn, kicking up dirt at Johnny and his car before driving to the track. The man cursed, wiping his window with the sleeve of his shirt before getting in and following after Zoey.

"She's not gonna win," Johnny's cousin said, walking alongside me as we made our way to where the others stood. I didn't want to bite, I especially didn't want to engage with anyone related to the asshole. But ...

"Why not?"

"Tires. She should've picked something with more traction for a dirt race. Probably didn't think it'd matter too much, since those tires are good for asphalt racing. And it wouldn't've mattered if she was going up against anybody else. But Johnny's pissed about everything she's done this month and the whole getting-fired thing. Thanks for that, by the way. I was totally looking forward to not having help pay off my mortgage."

"I found another woman's underwear in the garage." I didn't think I needed to defend myself, but I did want this guy to remember just how much of a dick his cousin is.

"Christ," the guy hissed and I quickened my pace to join the others to watch Johnny and Zoey race.

The crowd was standing a good 20 feet or so from the track, where Johnny and Zoey were parked, engines revving. A black spray-painted line marked the starting point and on the side closest to the crowd, was a camera set up on a tripod. Between the two racers was a woman with high hair and stereotypical short shorts. She held up a white and black checkered flag and everything went quiet. The crowd, the cars, everything. Then she brought it down and the sound erupted.

Zoey took off first, hitting the gas and taking the lead from Johnny with her hand flying out the window, middle finger up. My heart leaped into my throat as I watched her go. She might actually win this. She was going to win.

But then they hit the first turn and Zoey's tires skidded. The tail of the car swung across the dirt, the force nearly turning her the whole way around. Zoey righted the car quickly, but it cost her. Her lead was nearly gone.

With each turn, Johnny caught up bit by bit. Zoey's turns had gotten cleaner, with less dust flying into the air and no tire squealing, but in order to make those turns she had to slow down. Slow down far too much. It was going to cost her too much.

Despite her losing ground, the crowd predominantly cheered for Zoey. They screamed her name and cringed when she made a bad move. And for a moment, I was caught in that atmosphere, the idea that if you cheered hard enough, and shouted loud enough, the underdog would run. Surely these folks would stop if all hope was lost.

But at the last turn, with Zoey and Johnny neck and neck, he finally took the lead.

"Fuck, yeah!" Johnny shouted, sticking his head out the window as he crossed the finish line. The rest of the crowd groaned and I heard Johnny's cousin say something about how he'll be insufferable now.

My focus was on Zoey.

She'd stopped her car right at the finish line and was staring straight ahead, motionless. From where I stood, I couldn't even tell if she was blinking. She was frozen, trapped in that moment of loss, probably overthinking every single thing that went wrong and what she could have fixed. I needed to snap her out of it.

But I didn't get to her first. Johnny did.

The second I started to Zoey, Johnny hopped out of his car and strode over to her with a snide, disgusting smirk on his face. He went up to Zoey's side and tapped on the window. Zoey's shoulders tensed and she turned to roll the window down. There were some words exchanged that I wasn't close enough to catch, but when I stepped in front of the car I caught a glint of silver being chucked a Johnny.

"Got anything else you want to say?" Zoey asked, one corner of her lip up in a snarl.

"Nah, not as long as you keep out of my life," he sneered before holding out a ring of keys on his finger, swinging them in front of Zoey like he was trying to taunt her with them. It was working. Her face heated with a rage that had been missing these past few days. All of a sudden that murderous glint was back in her eyes.

"Go celebrate your win with someone who cares," I told him, rounding the hood of the car so I stood next to him, ready to push him away if he tried anything. When his gaze turned to me, his eyes sharpened, all his fury now aimed at me.

"You lost me my fucking job," he gritted taking a step towards me, one arm raised like he was about to return the black eye I'd given him. Too bad that hadn't affected his racing.

Zoey slammed on her gas, the revving much harsher than it had been before the race, and Johnny froze.

"Give me a fucking reason," Zoey said, head out of the window to glare at Johnny.

"Whatever," he grumbled, dropping his arm and backing away from me. "You're not worth the trouble anyways."

He said that last bit directly at Zoey and now it was my turn to step forward, ready for a fight.

"Just get in the car, Stephen." For a moment, I considered ignoring her and going after that prick. But there was a weariness in her tone that worried me. And I'd much rather spend my energy on Zoey than that asshole.

So I got in the car and Zoey drove us off the track. Then back to the road, not sparing a glance to the folks who waved and shouted their goodbyes.

"Are we not going to —"

"No. I just — I'd rather be back home."

"All right," I said, as softly as I could. I rested my hand on her bouncing knee. She stopped moving for a second before shaking me off.

"Should we try to kill him?" It shouldn't have been the first thing I offered, but her quiet anger demanded big actions. She hadn't said it out loud, but I knew this race was supposed to be the last thing that tied her to Johnny. Losing it must've hurt.

"Ha!" Zoey said the word instead of actually laughing. "Given that he just got my Miura, I'd be in jail in less than an hour of them finding the body."

"Miura?" I repeated.

"It's one of my old cars. Don't worry about it," she said, waving her hand in my direction.

"Sounds foreign," I noted and was rewarded with a real laugh, albeit a small one.

"Speaking of foreign cars, Dan said your part got there this afternoon. He's fixed up some pieces for you in between other customers, so I should be able to finish it off for you tomorrow afternoon. Then you can be on your way."

"Zoey, you don't have to rush it, I'm in no hurry to —"

"No, it's fine. I'll need something to keep my hands busy anyway. I'll probably be in the garage the rest of the night too. So don't wait up for me."

"Zoey —"

"Stephen, this isn't one of the times where you give me an hour and then follow up. I ..." Her grip on the wheel tightened and she took a deep, shaky breath. "I need more time than that."

I didn't like that this car ride felt like the first one. I didn't like that she wasn't able to let me hear what she was thinking. I didn't like that she was hurting and I couldn't do anything to stop it.

But I respected her need to think through things first. And waiting for her, to be ready for her when she needed me to be, would be as easy as breathing. Plus I had some thinking of my own to do. So I simply said, "Okay. I'll wait for you."

28

OWNING YOUR UNHINGED BULLSHIT

Zoey

The race taught me a few distinct life lessons.

Lesson one, don't underestimate a tire's roll in a race. When Stephen put on a different set of tires than I picked out, I didn't think it'd be that big of a deal. He'd picked a set that was good for racing on asphalt, so I figured they'd work just as well. Plus it meant a lot that he'd put the effort into researching that for me and I didn't want to undo that.

Lesson two, don't bet family heirlooms, no matter how pissed off you are. Back when Dad first got sick, Mom suggested selling a car or two to pay for his medical bills. Dad nearly had a heart attack over the suggestion. The fact that I was so blinded by anger to not have the same reaction should've been a sign I was too far gone.

Lesson three, assholes who have known you for far longer than they deserved to will know exactly what to say to make the deepest cut. "All you're petty little unhinged bullshit is gonna catch up to you one day. Lord know how much longer that one's gonna stick around for when you could turn on him next."

And he was right. I was an unhinged, petty bitch, and losing that race, seeing Johnny dangle my keys in front of my face, made me want to run him over. Not kill. Just maybe break his foot a little. If he had tried to do anything to Stephen, I would've done it. And I'm not completely sure if that action would have been driven by my anger or my feelings for Stephen.

And isn't that just fucking insane? I couldn't separate my anger from everything else. It was like an oil spill. And just when I thought I'd cleaned it all up, rescued and cleaned all the ducks with Dawn, I found a leak. And the leak caught fire and threatened to burn everything else down.

Last month, I would've been fine with everything burning. I would've said good riddance. But then some cute weirdo came into my life, looked at my unhinged anger, and said it was fine, expected even. He gave my anger space, affirmed it, and like hell was I gonna lose that just because I took things a step too far like I did betting a near million-dollar car. Just the thought of Stephen catching me over Johnny's dead body or something and drawing the line and leaving me made my stomach churn. Which was its own separate sort of crazy to have so many feelings for a guy I'd known for a month.

So it was time to get my shit under control. My unhingedness would be limited to controlled avenues and I wouldn't drag Stephen into anything else. I'd send him back to Seattle with a smile so he didn't worry about me being on my own and doing something dumb and reckless without him.

In hindsight, the long-distance thing was probably going to be good for us. He'd have some space from my craziness and realize if it was too much or not for a regular basis. And I wouldn't become a glutton for reliable orgasms and fall in love with him insanely fast because of it. And other things.

There were a lot of reasons to fall in love with Stephen for. And I was dangerously close to falling in love with that weirdo.

Which is why I needed to get him out of here before I hit his unhinged limit. Then I can do therapy or journaling or whatever that could help with my desire to break shit and murder people for looking at my weirdo wrong.

Plus Stephen hadn't been back home in god knows how long. There was probably shit he needed to do, routines he was anxious to get back to. Darren probably missed him too. So it was a good thing I was sending him off.

That twist in my gut was just dumb bullshit. Stephen said a long-distance thing would work, so it'll work. If anything, Stephen was the practical to my crazy. He'll probably be relieved when I bring up him going home.

"Zoey."

I looked up from the living room floor where I had spent the last half hour folding and refolding Stephen's clothes so everything would fit in his bag. Either he'd hidden a bag somewhere or he had some masterful way of folding because I couldn't get them to fit for shit.

"What're you doing with my things?"

"Well, since I finished up the last bit of work on your car last night, I figured I'd help you pack too."

"Why would I want you to do that?"

I took a beat, set down the shirt I was folding, and gave him a 'what the fuck' look.

"So that you can go home?" I said hesitantly. Stephen just kept staring at me like I was speaking a foreign language. "Look, last night sucked. And I could very easily see myself going back into a spiral of anger. But that doesn't mean you shouldn't go back home now that you can. I promise not to do any more TP-ing or breaking and entering. I'll deal with my bullshit somehow and you can go back to your life. We started things too quickly anyway, it's for the best that we take a break from crazy and start the long-distance thing. And I'm sure Darren's been worried about you, stuck in some small, unheard-of town. You should give me his number, by the way. I don't think it's fair that you have a group chat with my friends but not vice versa."

I was rambling and I hated it. Up until last year, I thought I was done being nervous over boys. Guess that was just another thing to be pissed about. Now I had to relive the nervous beginnings of a relationship. This time with a guy that lived on the other side of the country. Fun.

Stephen looked at his overfilled bag, then at me, his face unreadable. The anxious feeling doubled.

"Just — I don't know, respond already," I groaned, fighting the urge to nudge him out the door before he said anything I didn't want to hear.

"I can't do the long-distance thing anymore."

"Oh." That was exactly what I didn't want to hear.

Technically, I knew this was a possibility. I mean, we'd known each other for like a month. And I'd been doing stupid ass, petty shit the whole time. He'd have to be just as unhinged as me to want to keep this going. And I couldn't begrudge him for not being as crazy as me. I didn't like how crazy I felt.

"That's fine," I grumbled, standing and kicking at his suitcase. Not hard, just ... fuck. Logic was not making this feel any better. This was stupid, feelings were stupid. I don't want to feel anything ever again.

"Whoa, whoa. Wait a second." Stephen wrapped his arms around me and twisted me to face him. "I mean I can't do long-distance because that sounds absolutely miserable. Why would I want to go back to my lonely apartment, when I could just move in with you?"

"What?" There's no way I heard that right. "Why would you wanna move in with me?"

"Why wouldn't I?" was his immediate response.

"Um, because that's a crazy thing to do! Your whole life is back in Seattle and you're just gonna abandon it for some unhinged bitch? I literally just lost nearly a million dollars because I was pissed at my ex. You can't move across the country for that kind of crazy."

Stephen narrowed his eyes at me, hands moving from my waist to my elbows.

"What makes you say all that?"

"Other than the fact that it's all true?"

"All of it?" When I nodded his brow furrowed. "Why was one car worth that much? Could it fly?"

"It's old and rare and really fucking cool. And I was a dumbass for betting it. You can't move across the country for that level of dumbassery." I pushed his arms away and started shoving the rest of his things into the bag.

"Why not? I can work remotely. I'm only needed in Seattle a few days out of the year. I'd much rather spend my time here with you."

"No. You're not listening." I picked up the barely zipped bag and pushed it into his arms. "Moving here with me is not something you should just decide all willy-nilly. Go home. Cool off. And we can talk about it in a ... I dunno, a month or two. Would that be normal?"

"I don't care about normal. I care about you." He looked at his bag, pieces of clothing sticking out from the zipper. Then he looked at me, those eyes sparkling, searching. "Is there a real reason you want me to leave?"

I stared at him for a long time, going over several arguments in my head, trying to decide what logic he would listen to. Stephen just waited for me to speak, like he always did. So, with a sigh, I gave him the root answer.

"I'm not worth that sort of trouble. I need to stop being crazy and move on. *Then* we can talk about living together." Before the words were completely out of my mouth, Stephen's bag was on the floor and his arms wrapped around me.

"You're right. You're worth *so much more* than just moving across the country for. You feel like home to me, pretty girl. Crazy and all. The only way you'd get me to go is if you tell me you don't feel the same," he whispered and I hugged him back, clinging to him like a raft. "But Zoey, you don't have to 'stop being crazy' to move on. That's the part of you he didn't accept. You need to let it breathe and accept it as part of you, a great part of you. Then I think you'll start feeling better."

"What if I do something too crazy?"

"Zoey, I asked if you wanted to kill a man yesterday."

"You didn't mean that," I said, rolling my eyes even though my face was buried in his shoulder and I had no intention of moving. Because then he'd see I was crying all because he told me to keep being crazy. Like that one Taylor Swift song, Jeweled or something. I'd have to ask Olivia.

"I think I did mean it."

"Oh my god." I pulled back to look at him, half joking but half genuinely concerned. "I'm giving you my crazy. What's Darren gonna say?"

"No. That's not — why would you even care about what Darren would say? You haven't even talked to him yet. *I* don't care what Darren would say."

"He's your best friend, of course I care. My friends approve of our relationship, so I want him to approve too." I'd derailed this conversation into nonsense. I could tell Stephen knew it by the way his eyebrow tilted when I leaned back to look at him. But just like always, he was going to give me a moment.

"Darren will like you. He might think you're a little crazy, but he'll also know it's the kind of crazy I need. We'll probably make him worried though, since neither of us is great at texting back. He gives me a hard time about that, so I imagine he'll assume if both of us don't respond, we're dead in a ditch. Which isn't all that different from how he thinks now."

"Hmph. Fine. So Darren will probably be cool with it. But what about *you*? You're the one doing the insane, reckless thing. We should be questioning your sanity and motive?"

"My motive?" he repeated with a small chuckle. "That's easy, pretty girl. My motive is I love you and I wanna stay by your side."

"What? No, you don't." I laughed. Stephen didn't. "No fucking way."

Thankfully, that did get him to smile. So at least my reaction wasn't that much of a fuck up.

"Yes, I do. Does that prove I'm just as crazy as you and convince you to let me stay? I have a backup plan, if not."

"Back up plan?" I asked, because what the hell did that mean? Backup plan for what? When did he have time to think about that when he literally just brought up moving here?

I mean, I guess I just brought up him heading home. But that's completely different. We'd agreed on doing long-distance already, so obviously he was planning on going back.

"Does that mean you've been considering staying for a while now and I got all anxious about sending you home and being too much for nothing? Are you even, like, I dunno, second-guessing anything now that you know how much that car I lost was worth?"

"Not at all," Stephen said with a maddening smirk.

"Oh my god," I murmured, laughing from all the wasted frustration and worry. "You're actually crazier than me. That's no good, you're supposed to be the logical one, the one who keeps me from doing illegal shit."

"Well, I didn't do too well with that, now did I? Guess I should return the favor." He leaned over to kiss my cheek then spun on his heel and headed to the door. By the time I figured out that meant he was going off to do something stupid, he was already gone.

Too bad for that dumbass I knew exactly what kind of insane, grand gesture he'd try to pull.

Fuck I just might love him too.

29

HAPPILY EVER-AFTERS INVOLVE SLIGHT THIEVERY

STEPHEN

I had a lot of time to think last night since Zoey never came to bed. I thought about how she was probably pissed about the race, how that car probably meant more than she led on, and how the thought of going back to Seattle no longer sounded unpleasant but downright dreadful.

Deciding to stay in Snowfall was an easy decision. Figuring out how to convince Zoey it wasn't a crazy decision was harder.

I figured she'd say it was too soon, that it was rushing things. And while I could see that being a valid argument, it didn't hold any water when I saw her packing my clothes, tears in her eyes. I'm pretty sure she hadn't realized she was crying, she was just that damn stubborn.

She didn't want me to leave, so I wasn't leaving. It was as simple as that.

Except I hadn't expected her to think she wasn't worth the trouble or that her craziness could drive me away. Both things were so far from the truth that there was no universe I would've considered them a possibility.

But I could see the dots she was connecting. Johnny cheated on her for some reason. He'd definitely called her a crazy bitch in my presence, so who knew what else he'd said when I wasn't there. It very well could have been the reason he decided to cheat. And now Zoey thought it'd drive me away too.

Good thing I had just the plan to show her I could be just as crazy for her. And only her.

Step one of that plan was to get her girls together.

"Welcome to Dear Diner, just you today?" the hostess at Rosie's diner asked when I stepped in.

"Oh, no. Thank you. I'm here to see Rosie."

The girl took a big, dramatic breath, then shouted back to the kitchen for Rosie. No one else in the diner batted an eye at the girl's holler, but when Rosie stepped out from the kitchen, she smacked the girl's arm.

"What have I told you about acting up in the shop like that?" Rosie hissed to the hostess.

"What? It did bother anybody." The girl waved an arm around the diner and all the unbothered guests. Rosie narrowed a glare at her, saying something with the look that got the girl to quiet.

"Behave while I'm gone. Please," Rosie pleaded before turning to me with a pleasant smile that didn't match her attitude towards the girl. "Hey, Stephen. Ready to go?"

"Yes, but ..." I trailed off, curious about what that was about but not sure it was my place to ask.

"One of my sisters," she explained as we walked out of the diner. "It's a family business but the younger ones aren't too involved. Honestly, I prefer it that way. They have a tendency of ... making a mess of things."

"Huh. How many siblings do you have?" I asked.

"Oh, I'm the oldest of seven. Three girls, including me, and then the four boys."

"Dear lord," I murmured. I couldn't imagine having seven kids in one house. I don't think I could manage more than two. I know Zoey mentioned wanting kids at some point, I'd have to make sure we were on the same page about that.

"You know, Zoey told us you weren't a fan of small talk. And I'd say that was dangerously close," Rosie teased, nudging me with her elbow. "So, when'd you realize you loved her?"

"When I got back from punching Johnny for the underwear thing."

"Aw, that's so sweet," she crooned.

"Sweet?" I repeated.

"Well, yeah. You didn't realize you were in love until you're actions proved it. I like that sort of thing. Too many people say they love somebody without meaning it."

"Did —"

"Nope," Rosie said, voice a little too bright. "I didn't call in my siblings to watch my restaurant to gab about myself. We've got a heist to plan."

"I don't understand why we're sneaking around like this. One conversation isn't legally binding, so we —"

"Shush," Olivia said, tugging at Ashley so that she wasn't visible over the bush outside Johnny's cousin's house.

"But this is kind of ridiculous, I mean —"

"Says the woman who taped cardboard all over Mason's front windows?" Shea pointed out and Ashley immediately quieted. Apparently, today was quite the day for Ashley and Mason's rivalry. After she'd done the cardboard thing, he snuck into her shop through the back and pulled the plug on her fridge and she didn't notice until closing, which was just enough time to ruin her icings or something. Her ranting on the way here was a bit too quick for me to follow.

But fortunately, she had enough leftover scones that we could use for a fake delivery for Johnny.

"Ashley, come here for a second," Roxie said, gesturing for Ashley. When she went over, Roxie started rearranging Ashley's clothes and hair, even pulling out some lip gloss from nowhere.

"Is this really necessary?" Ashley asked.

"Probably not, but it's fun," Roxie said. "You've got this whole cute housewife vibe going on, which might do it for guys like Mason who want a family and a white picket fence. But Johnny's a pig and we need him distracted."

"I am not Mason's type," Ashley grumbled, to which all the girls hummed in disbelief.

When Roxie finished with Ashley, she made jazz hands before pushing Ashley towards the path to the front door. Ashley grumbled at Roxie but quickly straightened up and walked to the door, pastry box in hand.

The rest of us waited behind the bush, clambering and shushing each other so we could hear what was happening.

"Hi, I've got a delivery for Johnny," Ashley said, her voice perkier than usual. I caught some grumbling and peeked around the corner to see Ashley's posture loosen and her talking to herself like she was mocking whoever she'd spoken to. Then Johnny came into view and she straightened herself up with a bright smile. "Johnny, right?"

"Yeah. And who are you, mystery dessert girl?"

From behind me, Shea made a gagging noise. Olivia smacked her arm then took hold of her shirt and dragged her to standing. With Johnny distracted, we darted into the backyard. As quietly as the five of us could manage, we made our way to the back door and Olivia peaked into the window. She gave a thumbs up then, with the speed of a sloth, turned the door knob.

Door opened, we scrambled inside.

The back door led us to a kitchen ... a surprisingly modern kitchen. Butcher block countertops, a pot filler over the gas stove, and an industrial-sized mixer. It was the kitchen of a chef.

"Shit, I always forget Grant is some kind of professional chef. Should we try and hook Ashley up with him?" Shea asked, saying exactly what I had been thinking.

"And deny her eventual hate sex with Mason? Absolutely not," Roxie whispered.

"Oh no, I think her and Mason will figure it out soon," Rosie said.

"Uh-huh, and you're not just saying that because the date you bid on is coming up?" Shea asked.

"Bid?" I repeated.

"Yeah, there's a bidding board up at the community center for when Mason and Ashley finally get together. You'll see it when we go to town hall next week," Olivia answered.

"There're town halls?" I figured the festivals were the last of the small town stereotypes Snowfall was going to check off.

Rosie hushed us and began crawling past the counter and to the dining room table. She peered her head over the table and started sifting through the stack of papers there. The rest of us scattered to other parts of the house to search for the keys to Zoey's car.

Crouched and tiptoeing, I made my way down the hall to, presumably, the bedrooms. From the front door, I could hear Ashley's high-pitched laugh and Johnny's responding chuckle. He definitely thought she was interested in him and I wanted to gag. But instead, I cracked open the first door down the hall.

"Jesus fucking Christ," Johnny's cousin murmured, getting up from where he sat on his bed and crossing the room to loom over me at the door. "I'm too tired to give a shit about whatever you're up to, just leave me out of it."

The door slammed in my face and I thanked my lucky stars the guy had given up. Though that did little to calm my raging pulse. How the hell had Zoey managed to steal that other car without so much as looking nervous as she drove it around?

Once I'd finally caught my breath, I opened the next bedroom door.

The first thing that struck me as I crawled into the room was, it was definitely Johnny's. There were clothes strewn everywhere, across the floor, over the dresser, and balled up by the hamper. And there were car posters taped to the wall with women in bikinis. It was the room of a man-child. And it smelled like it.

The second thing I noticed was a woman's legs hanging down from the mattress.

"Shit." I skittered backward, falling on my ass.

The bed shifted as the woman stood and ...

"Zoey?" I nearly shouted. Zoey put a finger to her lips and with her other hand held up the keys.

"I figured this was the stupid shit you'd do to prove I'm not too crazy to love," she said, crouching down so we were level. "Too bad for you, I've got more car stealing experience."

Zoey reached a hand out for me and I took it, pulling her down on top of me. Hands sliding into her hair, I pulled her face to mine and kissed her. I kissed my crazy girl because of course she'd figure me out and do it on her own. But ...

"How am I supposed to prove I should stay now?" I asked, pulling away just enough so I could speak, my lips still grazing hers.

"Hmm. You mentioned something about me sitting on your face before. Is that still an option?"

My mouth instantly watered. If we were anywhere else, I would have laid back and pulled her on top of me. This wasn't the time or place. But … Ashley was supposed to keep Johnny occupied for a few more minutes. That should be enough time for me to get her wet, so that when she did climb on top of me —

"The fuck!" Johnny shouted, the door bursting open the rest of the way and knocking into the wall. "What? Is the next thing on your revenge plan to fuck on my bed?"

"Ew," Zoey said, her face wrinkling at the thought. She pushed back on her feet and stood, once again holding a hand out for me. This time I took her help and stood beside her, facing Johnny.

"Then what the fuck are you doing here?"

"Getting back what belongs to me." Zoey flashed the keys before sliding them into a back pocket. "And before you say anything about going back on my word, you went back on yours first and you never even said you were sorry. I even tried to make you, but that was just a waste of time. So with this, we'll call it even."

Zoey took my hand and started walking us away. In the hall the rest of the girls stood together, looking sheepish. When they saw Zoey, Shea nudged Roxie and the other woman just rolled her eyes. Olivia split from the group to hug Zoey and me.

"This was a stupid attempt at a heist, we got caught almost immediately," she mumbled to us. "I don't know how you managed all those unhinged plans on your own."

"I wasn't alone," Zoey said, looking around Olivia's head to smile at me. I squeezed her hand in return. She wouldn't have to do anything alone again.

"Would you get the fuck out of my house?" Johnny shouted from his room, the door shutting with a loud snap, like maybe he broke something. From his cousin's room, we heard one long groan. It gave me the impression that Johnny might not have a place to stay for much longer.

"Let's go, I've got the car and a man who appreciates my antics. There's nothing else I need here."

30

PAPER HEARTS BUT THIS TIME WITH FEELING

ZOEY

One year later

"I think it would make more logical sense if Ms. Taylor had the ones submitted last year all in one place," Stephen noted, squinting at one of the hundreds of thousands of paper hearts pinned all around downtown.

"I'm sorry, you've lived here for how long now and you still expect Ms. Taylor to have any sort of sense?" I asked, knocking my shoulder into his arm.

"Okay, fine. But you'd think somebody would have pointed out that it's hard to find your heart again the next year."

"Finding it is part of the fun," I told him, this time wrapping my arm around his and pulling him close. I looked around the festival, trying to catch sight of the others. We'd gotten a few additions this year with new partners and even Bailey had taken the trip to attend. But as soon as we'd done our heart for the year, they all disappeared into the crowd. Or maybe that was just because Stephen dragged us away to look for last year's heart. "I don't even remember what I wrote, do you?"

Stephen stiffened beside me.

"Oh my god, you do remember? What was it?" I grabbed at the front of his shirt, shaking him.

"You'll see when we find it," he grumbled, quickening his pace as we headed to the gazebo. I damn near tripped over my feet trying to keep up with him.

When we got to the gazebo, Stephen pushed me towards the steps. "You look in there, I'll look around the railings."

"All right, weirdo," I muttered, taking the steps to enter the magic heart cloud the gazebo had been transformed into. With a gentle hand, I sifted through the hearts, finding familiar names and sweet messages.

Then, in the center, I found ours. I twisted the string around to read what we'd written.

On my side, I'd put *you were exactly what I needed, thank you.*

And on Stephen's side, he'd written *it's not going to take much longer for me to fall in love with you, pretty girl.*

"Hey, Stephen, I found —" I turned back to the exit to get my weirdo, only to find him right there, kneeling.

"Will you marry me?" He held up a band with little diamonds embedded like stars. It wouldn't get caught on anything while I'm working and there was less of a chance the gems would get scratched. It was perfect and clearly thought through.

"Don't you think it's a little crazy to get engaged after just a year?" I teased, holding out my hand and pulling him up. Stephen took the ring out of the box and slid it onto my finger without me having to say yes. He already knew the answer.

"No. I thought about marrying you last year. But waiting until today seemed more romantic. I tried to get Clive involved, but that deer is selectively food-motivated."

"Oh my god, take the ring off. I won't accept it until you get Clive here."

Stephen, still holding my hand, lifted an eyebrow. I kept my face straight just long enough for him to sigh and move to take off the ring. Then I pulled my hand away, grabbed him by the collar, and kissed him.

From outside the gazebo, a series of shouts and whistles sounded. I looked over to see all my friends, my mom, and even Darren gathered there, all smiling and cheering for us.

"You got Darren here, but you couldn't get Clive?" I teased.

"I'll get him for the wedding. Promise."

"All right, but I'm holding you to that. If Clive's not there, you're gonna have a runaway bride."

"Pretty girl, I've done my best to set up this nice romantic moment. Can you please stop talking about the damn deer?" Stephen groaned, resting his forehead on mine.

"But without Clive, we never would have met," I pointed out, tapping a finger on his chest. Stephen sighed and pressed a soft kiss to my lips.

"Clive will be there," he promised.

"Have I mentioned I love how you let me be crazy?" I whispered, kissing him with renewed energy. We wouldn't be staying at the festival much longer if I had any say in it.

31

***

WISHING FOR AN EVASIVE DEER

STEPHEN

Four months later

"Hey, Stephen, we've got … a problem," Eli said, stepping into the groomsman side of the church/community center.

"It's Clive, isn't it?" I know Zoey loved this fucking deer to death, that he was a main cause of her income, but I wanted to murder him. No, not murder him. I wanted to tell Zoey he married a deer in the next county and moved there. That didn't sound insane, right?

"Yeah, he *was* following the carrot trail, but then … I dunno, he got distracted by something."

"Zoey wouldn't *really* run if the deer wasn't here, right?" Dennis asked, placing what I'm sure was supposed to be a comforting hand on my shoulder.

"No, she would." All of my groomsmen made a sympathetic oof.

"I really don't understand what the big deal is about this deer," Darren said, picking at the lint on his suit.

"Then you can go get him," I told him, shoving the extra bag of corn I had tucked in my pocket at Darren's chest.

"Seriously? We're going out in ten."

"Yeah. And if it's between you and the deer missing the wedding, I'd rather it be you."

Darren stared at me for a long moment before he finally sighed and went off, grumbling the whole way out the door.

"I'll go help him look, I'm sure we'll find him, before taking off" Eli said, clapping a hand on my shoulder . Eli was an optimistic man, it made him a good friend but it was a trait I couldn't appreciate in the moment. Especially when Darren hadn't come back by the time I was pushed out the door and to the gazebo by the wedding planner.

I stood there, debating my choices. Zoey was just stubborn enough to run off if Clive wasn't in attendance. We were already legally married, so ruining the ceremony wouldn't matter too much. And I assume she'd come back for the reception after following through with her dramatics. But ...

The music shifted and Zoey came into sight. She was stunning in the white lace, a long train flowing behind her, sleeves that dipped to the floor. And beside her, on a leash, was Clive.

The crowd, the bridal party, and even the priest were all stifling laughter as Zoey walked down the aisle with Clive by her side. But I couldn't help myself. I threw my head back, laughing. And when my beautiful bride stepped up by my side, she was laughing too. A beautiful cackling laugh that, when she dropped the leash to take my hand, sent Clive skittering away.

"How'd you manage that, pretty girl?" I whispered, using her hand to pull her close so I could press a kiss to her veiled forehead.

"My bachelorette party might've involved some lasso lessons with the resident cowboy."

"Mhmm, so that's why you were out so late that night?"

"Well, yeah. I didn't want to risk you not getting him here. Then I'd have to run away and these shoes aren't great for that." She kicked out one leg from the flowing fabric to show a pastel blue flat. "I mean, I guess if I had to run, I could. But I'd get blisters for sure."

"God, I love your crazy, pretty girl." I pressed another kiss to her forehead and she halfheartedly smacked my chest.

"Shush, we're not to the kissing part yet."

Your next

Snowfall Valley

Era

Ashley Bowen

The Other Side Of The Door

Taylor Swift

K.E. Monteith is an anxious hot mess that writes about people like her fall in love and get spicy. You'll usually find her talking about her dogs, complaining about chronic pain, or screaming about something DropOut related or her current hyper fixation.

Sign up for her newsletter for bonus scenes, giveaways, and more.